Playing with Shadows

ILLINOIS SHORT FICTION

A list of books in the series appears at the end of this volume.

Gloria Whelan

Playing with Shadows

UNIVERSITY OF ILLINOIS PRESS

Urbana and Chicago

Publication of this work was supported in part
by grants from the National Endowment for the Arts
and the Illinois Arts Council, a state agency.

Some of these stories were written with the help
of a grant from the Michigan Council for the Arts.

This book is printed on acid-free paper.

"A Lesson in the Classics," *Ontario Review,* Summer 1983
"Spies and Lovers," *Passages North,* Winter 1981
"A Dwelling Place for Dragons," *Michigan Quarterly Review,* Summer 1983
"Beneath the Fig Trees," *Michigan Quarterly Review,* Summer 1981
"Sympathy Notes," *Virginia Quarterly Review,* forthcoming
"First Light," *Detroit Monthly,* September 1987
"The Dogs in Renoir's Garden," *Virginia Quarterly Review,* Winter 1983
"The Mummies of Guanajuato," *Story Quarterly,* Tenth Anniversary Issue 1985
"Two Are Better Than One," *Passages North,* Summer 1983
"The Showing," *Passages North,* Winter 1987
"The Secret Meeting with Mr. Eliot," *The Missouri Review,* Winter 1983
"Keeping House with Freud," *The Gettysburg Review,* January 1988

Library of Congress Cataloging-in-Publication Data

Whelan, Gloria.
    Playing with shadows.

    (Illinois short fiction)
I. Title. II. Series.
PS3573.H442P53   1988   813'.54   87-35690
ISBN 0-252-01524-X

For my mother,
Hildegarde Rewoldt

Contents

A Lesson in the Classics   1

Spies and Lovers   16

A Dwelling Place for Dragons   23

Children in the Park   30

Beneath the Fig Trees   42

Playing with Shadows   49

Sympathy Notes   64

First Light   74

The Dogs in Renoir's Garden   85

The Mummies of Guanajuato   95

Two Are Better Than One   106

The Showing   115

The Secret Meeting with Mr. Eliot   124

Keeping House with Freud   133

A Lesson in the Classics

Walter Miller, paper and pencil in hand, awaited the English couple's order. "The Shrimp in Lemon Sauce," he addressed their indecision, "is a cold dish. The Shrimp Theseus is baked with feta cheese and a tomato sauce. Theseus, you will recall, came here to Crete to kill the Minotaur. He was the father of Hippolytus by the Queen of the Amazons. Later he married Phaedra. . . ." He tried to keep his tone light, gossipy, but the eyes of the couple glazed over as his students' eyes often had when he had tried to impart to them the differences between genuine and spurious diphthongs or the reasons the Ionic alphabet triumphed over the Attic. He sighed. There was, after all, little difference between his former position as professor of classical languages and his present one as maitre d' of the Poseidon.

The young couple, pale and delicate as two spring shoots, shivered in their flimsy holiday clothes. The early spring evenings in Agios Nikolaos could be cool. Winter snows still lay in crumpled folds on Mt. Dikti's summit, and the winds sweeping in from the Aegean were the temperature of a properly chilled white wine.

After the couple settled for the Shrimp Theseus, Professor Miller moved on to a table of Germans who began giving their order in a pastiche of pidgin English and Greek. When Professor Miller replied in his pedantic German, they lapsed gratefully into their own tongue, even teasing him a little, accusing him of learning his German from *Faust,* which was true.

The Café Poseidon looked out over the harbor to the nearby island of Spinalonga, where an imposing Venetian fortress had once enclosed a colony of lepers from Crete. Professor Miller wondered what it would be like to be exiled at the threshold of one's home—he, at least, had the grace of distance. Directly in front of the café, a row of fishing boats lay at anchor, painted in primary colors, their decks heaped with saffron-colored nets. Beyond the boats and the island were sea and mountains. Before his retirement he had lived for thirty years in a small college town in a prairie state. The sea and the mountains appeared to him a kind of boast or excess on the part of the Maker.

Professor Miller carried his orders to the kitchen. The taking of the orders and the settling of bills were his only responsibilities. The waiters, Evangelos and Stephanos, did the rest. They were aided by Evangelos's two school-girl cousins, Maria and Olga, who hovered about the table like mute butterflies, emptying ashtrays, brushing away crumbs, and giggling helplessly (Maria) or fleeing in panic (Olga) when a customer made a request of them.

The chef greeted him cheerfully, "Professor, the moussaka is from lunch and if you don't push it, it will be for lunch tomorrow." The farmer who delivered the eggs and cheese was having an ouzo. Professor Miller could smell the pungent mix of licorice from the drink and goat dung from the farmer's boots.

"Professor," the farmer said, "are you from New Jersey? I have a brother in New Jersey who cleans rugs. You call him up, and in five minutes he's there with his machine." Professor Miller tried to explain that more than a thousand miles lay between New Jersey and his own state, but the farmer refused to believe anything in America was beyond his brother's grasp. As the professor left the kitchen the farmer called after him, "You let me know when you're ready to go home—I'll send some cheese back for my brother. He'll take care of your rugs, cheap."

Professor Miller could not say when he would go home. He had first come to the Café Poseidon as a patron, choosing an outdoor table where, in his loneliness, he might have for company the people strolling along the sidewalk and the cars coming and going in the street. He and his wife, Connie, had planned the trip to Greece to celebrate his retirement as head of the classical language department at the small denominational college where he had taught Greek and Latin to a dwindling number of students—the ones going on to the seminary. The students at his college were romantics who refused to listen to the interminable history of man's bungling. They preferred to believe in a world where charity and love prevailed, and why should they not? They lived their lives in the company of good people, people who would willingly work against their own interest for the sake of a friend or a principle: from this they posited the rest of the world.

Professor Miller thought himself more sophisticated than the other members of the faculty, adopting for himself the role of ambassador from a wider, larger world: teaching the New Testament, but slipping in a little Aeschylus and even Aristophanes and then worrying that he was introducing the apple into Eden.

When five months before he and Connie were to leave for Greece, Connie had died, Professor Miller had decided to give the trip up, only to reconsider, alarmed by the way the objects in his home had grown leaden and immobile—the dregs from his pipe stayed in the ashtray, strata of soiled shirts and socks waited on the bedroom chair, even the airy tiers of used Kleenex that mounded alongside his bed would not disappear. When Connie had been alive, all these things had vanished the moment he put them down. With Connie gone, he had been afraid to settle into a chair or lie down on his bed for fear he, too, would remain rooted.

And so he had set off on the trip, conscientiously retaining in his itinerary Connie's preferences for settings rich in botany. His colleagues had envied his opportunity to follow in Paul's footsteps but his own interests centered on the archaeological sites, especially the realms of the doomed Atreus and Pelops families, whom he knew so well from the years of teaching and whose penchant for misfortune had always seemed to him at once fascinating and perverse.

In Athens, in Delphi, in Mycenae, rising early, climbing in and out of the tour buses, he had had little time for loneliness. He found his days full of confirmation. It was all there: the Stoa of Zeus where Socrates had paced, chivying his students; the mottled rose and gray rocky mound of the Areopagus where Paul had preached, with indifferent success, to the Athenians; the great lion gates inside which Clytemnestra had awaited Agamemnon, dagger in hand. He had climbed to the amphitheater atop the ruins of Delphi and, looking out over gray-green olive groves and flowering Judas, had seen, like a revelation, the line stretching straight—Yahweh, Zeus, Agamemnon, Socrates, Paul. He

had been right to fight the faculty, right to reject the word *pagan,* right
to insist on teaching it all. He took to having a glass of wine with his
dinner, feeling a mischievous relief that in these foreign parts, he was
free of the faculty's censorship.

On that first visit to the Poseidon, he had overheard one of the waiters trying unsuccessfully to explain to an Englishwoman why he was
unable to serve the woman's small son fresh milk. The professor, who
had conscientiously studied modern Greek in preparation for his trip,
excused himself for intruding and translated for the Englishwoman the
waiter's explanation that in Greece all was rock and drought; where
there was little pasture, there would be few cows.

Returning to dine at the Poseidon the evening before he was to leave
Crete, he had again come to the waiter's aid. A French family wanted
mineral water in place of the carafe of water that had been brought to
their table. Grateful for the professor's help, the waiter, whose name he
later learned was Evangelos, had presented Professor Miller with a
bottle of Demestica, explaining that their maitre d', who understood
these various languages, had left for Athens and a job in his uncle's
restaurant. Evangelos was a beautiful young man with tousled black
curls and a body that might have been sculpted by Phidias. There was a
sensuality about him and a sleek, pampered look suggesting women
spoiled him. At the same time, he had an ingratiating bonhomie which
Professor Miller, who had not had the opportunity to make friends with
a Greek on the trip, appreciated. When Evangelos said laughingly to
the professor, "Why don't you apply for the job of maitre d'?" Professor Miller had been pleased rather than insulted at the little joke.

That night he had returned to his hotel room and had begun to pack
his clothes. He was still tipsy from the bottle of wine, and the packing
did not go well. He sank down on his bed and, smiling foolishly, said
aloud, "Beware of Greeks bearing gifts." He had not been drunk since
his junior year at college, when he and his roommate, now the pastor
of a large congregation in Minneapolis, had stolen a bottle of his
grandfather's schnapps.

He thought of the musty smell that would greet him when he returned to his silent, empty house. Only that morning he had received a
letter telling of a late spring blizzard rolling across the prairie. He
decided he did not want to leave Greece with its sun and its hillsides

that had grown gold with blossoming brooms and heathers. Yet he did not wish to stay on alone at his hotel with no one to talk with and nothing to occupy him. Furthermore, his funds were dwindling.

The next morning he had walked over to the Poseidon and asked to see the owner. Evangelos, who was sitting over a cup of coffee in the empty restaurant, slowly thrust out his legs and stretched his arms like a cat who has been sleeping in the sun. He grinned at the professor. "Her office is just down the street," he said, "but you won't find her in for another hour. She likes her bed." He winked.

Professor Miller sat on the stony beach and watched enviously as an older couple rubbed one another's shoulders with suntan lotion. When an hour had passed, he walked down to the office Evangelos had pointed out. He found the proprietor of the restaurant, Madame Papoulias, who also managed a real estate firm and a travel agency. When he was admitted to her office, Professor Miller saw that although she was at least ten years younger than he was, her features were ancient. He had seen the same face, with its classic straight nose and dark oval eyes that tilted ever so slightly, peering out at him from Minoan murals in the museum at Iraklion. He felt he was entering another time.

As if the woman could read his mind, she had said, "I can see you are interested in seeing the less well known ruins—Phaestos or perhaps Petsofas or Zakros—someplace where a little still remains for the imagination. You think the Englishman Evans went too far with his reconstructions at Knossos: all that plaster and concrete offends you. I have a tour just for scholars like yourself and this early in the season I can give you a very good price."

He had been taken aback. It was not as a scholar that he wished to present himself. "I'm afraid that is not why I am here." She had spoken to him in English, but he replied in Greek, "I would like to be considered for the position of maitre d' at your restaurant, Madame. I must admit to having been a college professor all my life—although as a student I did wait on tables in a dormitory. However, I speak English, Greek, Italian, and German. My French is rudimentary, but the French neither expect nor want others to speak their language well. I am reliable and will not ask for much in the way of a salary."

Madame Papoulias had laughed out loud. This professor with his stilted Greek and fussy manner was a gift from the gods. The night before, two customers had refused to pay after Evangelos had botched their orders. In her mind she had already dressed the professor in the sea-blue jacket that was the uniform of her Poseidon employees. With his silver hair and fine carriage, he would give the restaurant dignity. Evangelos needed a little keeping down as well; he was taking too much for granted. She hired the professor on the spot and at considerably less than she would have had to pay her competitor's maitre d', whom she was planning to lure away. She also rented the professor a small studio apartment at only a slightly higher rent than she could have had from English tourists. The English infuriated her by taking long daily showers that exhausted the water reservoir.

Professor Miller knew he was being taken advantage of, but he did not mind; he was relieved to find himself in capable hands.

The next evening, compressed into a jacket that was too tight around his waist, and with the menu memorized in four languages—the work of a few hours—Professor Miller embarked upon his new profession. He imagined how horrified the faculty at his college would be were they to learn what he was doing, but he told himself there was nothing undignified in overseeing the serving of food; something the disciples themselves had once done. The waiters, Evangelos and Stephanos, were won over at once. Unlike the last maitre d' or any maitre d' of their memory, the professor scrupulously divided his tips with them. If they thought him a fool for doing so, they kept it to themselves.

Professor Miller was delighted with his small whitewashed room with its four arched windows that looked out onto the pebbled beach and the sea. The room was furnished with two narrow beds, a chest of drawers, a rough wooden table and chairs, and a soiled flokati rug that crouched on the floor like a matted sheep. A light bulb shaded by a cheese basket illuminated the room, imprinting an intricate lattice on the whitewashed wall. The room was equipped with a small refrigerator and a hot plate. Dishes had to be washed in the bathroom sink. The supply of water from the bathroom faucets was limited, but there was always an inch or so of water on the stone floor from a leak, whose source, like a hidden spring, he could never discover.

Each morning Professor Miller went first to the bakery for a cakelike bread seeded with raisins and then on to the square to buy oranges and a creamy sheep's cheese, mizithra, which he learned to eat as the Cretans did, with honey. After breakfast he boarded one of the buses that traveled between the villages. Some days he would take the coastal road, getting off at the seaside and walking for miles along the rocky shore, gazing out at the sea as if he expected Jason and the Argo to heave into view.

Other days he chose the road that wound up the mountain to the Lassithi plateau, passing through villages that clung like swallows' nests to the mountain. Each house had a roof piled high with drying brush to fuel the winter fires and a yard with rosebushes and goats. The rosebushes in the impoverished villages puzzled him; he had never thought of roses as a necessity.

Leaving the bus, he would wander out onto the meadows of the plateau, noting, for Connie's sake, the flora—pink anemones, lavender columbine, red poppies, and one day, a miniature white cyclamen with delicate, swept-back petals, like a child's pale face turned to the wind. There were apple and almond orchards and fig trees, whose immature fruit was like small, green amphorae. One morning he watched transported as the villagers set the sails on the thousands of windmills that pumped water into their parched fields. For a moment as the acres of canvas billowed out, he thought the whole plain would levitate.

In letters to his friends at the college, Professor Miller explained he was staying on to do some translating, which, he told himself, was not really a lie. Each morning about the time he used to leave for his first class, he caught himself thinking of the college—the long corridors that reeked from their nightly applications of ammonia and disinfectant, the worn linoleum floors and blemished walls, the students wearing T-shirts with pictures of Kierkegaard (seminary students) or C. S. Lewis (literature majors). He supposed the postcards he sent would be tacked up on the bulletin boards next to requests for roommates (neatness counts, charismatic preferred) and appeals to support missionaries aspiring to Uganda and Zaire.

He asked himself if in all his years of teaching he had made an impression on any of these students. He supposed so, for graduates had regularly returned to visit him. After a half hour's desultory conversation about the student's new life and the pursuits of his classmates, the student would fall silent and stare into space. Absorbing what? The books on his shelves? His faith? His love? Professor Miller shuddered. At the end of a half hour—or hour, if there were a greater need—the student, apparently replenished, would leave. Professor Miller sighed over these memories and told himself he must not look back, but looking forward was no better.

By late afternoon he was at the Poseidon for his dinner before going on duty. It was a pleasant time. Around the table they were a family. This evening Evangelos had teased, "You've got a woman. I see you get on the bus every day. Her husband goes off to the fields and you sneak in for a little party." He made a quick, obscene gesture which the professor did not understand. Olga and Maria blushed. The chef had reproved Evangelos, "You're not one to talk, a young roaster like you spending your nights with an old stewing hen." At this, Olga and Maria had a fit of giggling.

Lately Madame Papoulias had been joining them for dinner. Professor Miller was uncertain about her marital status. At first he thought her a widow, for she invariably wore black, but she explained, "It is only for a cousin, and one I never got on with, but the church expects you to wear mourning for three years. As you grow older, you are always in black." Her black sweater and skirt were comforting to Professor Miller, an outward confirmation of his inward state, for he could not stop thinking of his wife.

Madame Papoulias was a woman with a sensuous appetite, eating as though she were putting food to a use for which it was not intended. This evening she had come early and prepared *lagos,* hare, for them. Professor Miller watched with alarm as she lifted the delicate bones to her mouth and stripped off their meat. She might have borne a personal grudge against the small animal. When she caught him staring at her, he hastened to compliment her on the stew. She replied that she could do much better and invited him to her apartment for lunch the following Sunday.

In the intervening days he struggled with a growing sense of guilt, thinking it might be unsuitable for him to call at the apartment of Madame Papoulias. He had noticed the hungry way she had looked at him. Yet how often he and Connie had visited the homes of his fellow faculty members on Sunday afternoons, listening to classical record-ings, enjoying a potluck dinner, and always—for it was Sunday—ending the day with a short devotional service. Perhaps the Greeks had a similar tradition?

He was reassured when Madame Papoulias, a picture of suffering dignity, greeted him in her usual black clothes. But when he discovered he was to be the only guest, he grew uneasy and looked nervously about for clues as to what might happen to him. The apartment was furnished with cumbersome Victorian tables and chairs rooted like thick trees to the floor. On the walls were Kalim rugs and Cretan embroideries. The most prominent spot was given to an enormous tele-vision set, and arranged in front of the set was a pile of brightly colored cushions. Professor Miller thought the apartment a bit Gypsyish.

"There is no reason we should both be alone on a Sunday after-noon," Madame Papoulias said. It was late in May and hot weather had come. Sultry air found its way through the closed shutters and mingled but did not mix with the cool air trapped in the night by the thick walls.

When she poured him a glass of *tiskoudia,* which he knew to be Cretan gin, he covertly reconnoitered the potted plants, like a character in the hackneyed plot of a spy story, for one where the gin might be disposed of while his hostess was out of the room. Something warned him he must keep a clear head.

"Tell me," she said, "why an educated man like yourself has taken such a job, though God knows it was a blessing for me."

"I wanted to stay on here for a while. I've grown very fond of your island. And to be truthful, I didn't want to go back to an empty house." He explained about Connie, embarrassed to be mentioning her name in this woman's apartment.

"You are welcome to keep me company anytime. I don't eat enough when I cook for myself. Just see how thin I'm getting." She pushed in her stomach and threw out her ample chest.

Professor Miller felt his face grow red and reached for the gin.

After lunch they sat side by side on the cushions in front of the television set, watching a soccer match from Athens. Madame Pa-poulias, an enthusiast, nudged him with her elbow and grabbed at his thigh in her excitement. The game, incomprehensible to Professor

Miller, dragged on. When for a moment he nodded, she put her hand on his and suggested, "You needn't go in to the Poseidon; Evangelos can manage for one night."

The professor hastened off.

By July the water in the reservoirs was at a precarious level. Intrusive, scorching winds blew open the door and windows of Professor Miller's apartment. It was too hot to wander in the fields, and the reflection of the sun on the water made him giddy. He took to reading in his room until noon and then proceeding to Madame Papoulias's apartment for lunch, taking with him a basket of figs. They dined on cheese and salads. For dessert they ate the figs. Professor Miller watched squeamishly as the juice from the ripe fruit ran down Madame Papoulias's chin.

She spoke to him of the property she owned: on Koundourou Street, on Atlandithos Square, even a little house on the Plastira that looked out onto Lake Voulismani. "The view is superb, but the roof needs a bit of repair. My sister's son is working on it. He is a fisherman but he hasn't had his boat out all month. There aren't enough fish to pay for the gasoline. I don't understand it. The whole sea and there are no fish. It's another curse on Crete. We are an unlucky island."

Professor Miller demurred, "I doubt there is a more beautiful place on earth—the sky, the mountains" (he made a little halting gesture with his hand to indicate expanse), "the sea—whether there are fish in it or not."

"How happy I am to hear you, an American, say that. What I want is to find a way to get your people over here. The English and the Germans are the only ones who come. They have money, but they don't spend it. The Americans don't have the money, but they spend it anyhow."

Professor Miller was not accustomed to speak of money. The faculty at his college were poorly paid—as anyone should be, their president pointed out, who had undertaken a life of witness. The few businessmen he knew were alumni of the college, whom he had met while a member of the college gifts committee, and he knew them in the context of their wishing to give money away.

Madame Papoulias mistook his silence. "You are a deep one," she said. "I have decided you are working at the Poseidon to learn the restaurant business. Now that you are retired, you are going back to the States and will open a Greek restaurant. You are here to learn my little secrets." She waggled a finger at him.

For a moment he was charmed by the ridiculous idea and then, of course, denied it.

One afternoon when no breeze came through the shutters and even the lettuce leaves on the salad plates were limp, Madame Papoulias insisted Professor Miller remove his shoes and trousers and take a nap in her large mahogany bed. "You have to follow the custom of the country," she said, relaxing the knot on his tie and then turning her back to him so he might fiddle with her zipper. "In this weather you cannot remain on your feet all night if you don't take a little rest during the day." She lay beside him in a bra and petticoat of some slippery pink material. They were too small for her so that her flesh appeared even more abundant. He was being offered a second helping before he had begun on the first.

When her warm hand slipped into the fly of his shorts quick as a mouse into its hole, he wanted to grab his clothes and run. The word "fornicator" sounded in his head like a siren. Only a week before he had read in an Athens newspaper of a woman tourist from Australia and a married man from Athens who had been discovered in bed together and sent to jail. But running away would surely be an insult to Madame Papoulias. As they had all of his life, his manners prevailed.

Wherever he touched Madame Papoulias, her soft, moist flesh clung to him. What if as a punishment, he worried, their bodies were eternally bonded? Unlike his own God, who was merely strict, the Greek gods were capricious as well, and might they take precedence here?

Afterward he wondered if he were expected to whisper words of love, but she spoke instead of the villas and small hotels she would someday buy and refurbish. "There will certainly be more trouble in the Middle East and the cost of fuel will rise in England and Germany. It will become colder and colder for those people. They will come here to Crete, happy to pay large sums for the warmth of our sun." Her voice was husky with desire, but whether for him or for her future holdings, he could not say.

One afternoon she told him how it had been during the war. The day the Germans had parachuted into Crete she had been thirteen. She had looked up to see the sky full of white sails. "The sails of the windmills," she said, "to you are beautiful, but all I think of when I see them are the white sails in the sky when the Germans came down upon us."

At night as he lay alone in his own bed, pleasantly tired from an evening's work at the Poseidon, Professor Miller thought of Paul scourging the Corinthians for their lasciviousness. But the next day he would return to Madame Papoulias's apartment. It was not her flesh that brought him, for it had become an embarrassment to him that on most days he was capable of little more than companionship. He was attracted to Madame Papoulias's easy familiarity with tragedy and her ability to survive it. Her father had been accused by the Germans of sabotage. She and her mother had seen him taken off to be executed. During the occupation, many people in their village had starved. Yet here she was, triumphantly alive and flourishing, seeing opportunity in the disaster of nations growing cold.

Each time her warm skin grafted itself to his body, one more of life's abrasions healed over. Each time he entered her, he felt himself floundering in a great sea, while bit by bit the flotsam and jetsam of her vigor accumulated around him, so that at last he had enough to cling to, enough to bring him safely to shore. He watched her secretly, afraid he would find her growing weaker, fading as her strength flowed into him. But no, she remained as indomitable, as robust as ever. Gradually he found his thoughts creeping beyond Connie's death and his retirement. Exposed to the high sun of this woman, the shadows of his own sorrow grew shorter.

October was mild and pleasant but nothing green remained. The vegetation on the hillsides had withered and crisped. Everything had been harvested. The countryside was used up. Each day there were fewer tourists. Stephanos had been let go for the season. Olga and Maria had returned to school. Lying in bed beside Madame Papoulias one afternoon, he asked her if it was not time for him to leave as well. In her dresser mirror he could see the two of them stretched out like twin effigies on some ancient tomb. The effigy that was Madame Papoulias abruptly sat up.

"But November is our best month," she pleaded. "The sea still holds the warmth of the summer. With the tourists gone, the island is ours again. Forgive me for saying so, but what do you go back to? If you want a restaurant (Professor Miller had not been able to disabuse her of the idea), why not stay here? Send for your money. I know a way to get it into the country. It will go further here. With your capital, we can make the Poseidon a first-class restaurant, and next door there is a little hotel for sale. We could go in together." She padded over to the dresser and pulled some papers from a drawer. "Look, I have figured out how much you would have to put in. I promise you'll get your money back ten times over.

"You, professor, will tell me what Americans like, what they must have to make them comfortable. But of course we cannot make them *too* comfortable. They like to brag a little about being in a primitive country. Isn't that so? In exchange for American dollars we will make them a little comfortable and a little uncomfortable—you will tell me how much of each. You can write to your friends at the college and urge them to come. We will give them special rates."

Professor Miller saw that all those afternoons when they had been lying together, she had been planning how he might be used. This did not disturb him, for he was relieved to find he had not been alone in his need. What alarmed him was a vision of Professor Schuler, who taught Old Testament history, or Professor Liebig, who taught Christian ethics, and the head of the college, President Riess, lounging about on Madame Papoulias's cushions or gathered about her large mahogany bed observing Madame in her slippery petticoat and himself in his white shorts. He told himself he must leave at once.

That evening in the restaurant, Evangelos said, "I suppose you'll be going soon, Professor, like all the tourists." There was an unexpected note of satisfaction in his voice.

The professor, goaded by Evangelos's tone and unhappy at being lumped with the tourists, began to ask himself if he had to leave. When he was finished for the evening, instead of going to his room, he walked along the sea, dismayed that for all its expanse, a plane could carry him over it in no time, and not only through space, but through time as well. It would take him away from this ancient place that was the work of centuries to a countryside that was raw with newness. A thin edge of rose and turquoise separated sky from sea when he made the decision to sell his house. He need not even go home, where he would be sure to lose his resolve. He knew a lawyer who would take care of the business for him. With the money from the sale, he and Madame Papoulias would open the hotel, and of course they must marry. He recalled Jacqueline Kennedy's wedding to Onassis. On the day of their marriage would Madame Papoulias at last be allowed to discard her black clothes for a white dress? The President's widow had looked charming with a wreath of flowers in her dark hair. Perhaps Madame Papoulias would wear a similar wreath?

Professor Miller, pleasantly startled by his boldness, decided to go to Madame Papoulias's at once and tell her his news. He hurried past empty cafés and silent houses. Her street was approached by a flight of steep stairs. As he reached the top he was breathing very fast but whether from excitement or exhaustion he could not say. As he paused for a moment to catch his breath, he looked tenderly at Madame Papoulias's house. The white walls were stained with the spreading rose of morning sky. Blue shutters covered the windows. The small balcony was crowded with pots of sprawling red geraniums. He thought with pleasure: this will be my home.

At that moment, the door of Madame Papoulias's home opened and Evangelos stepped out. One hand was smoothing down his dampened curls, the other was making a little adjustment in the fit of his trousers. He saw Professor Miller and walked without hesitation toward him. Evangelos put an arm lightly around the professor, who had neither the pride nor the presence to step aside. The expression on Evangelos's sleep-swollen face was intimate and conspiratorial, like someone in a secret fraternity who at last has been permitted to identify himself to a fellow member. "I don't mind, Professor. We have a saying here, 'When the wine is good, you keep it for yourself; when it grows a little sour, you are glad to share it.' "

Professor Miller waited until Evangelos was out of sight before he descended the stairway into the street below. In the bakery, a man was sliding trays of bread onto the countertop. A few chairs in the cafés were already occupied by old men who wished not to be alone in the first hours of the day. He hurried on to his apartment and with shaking hands began to fold his clothes into tidy packages and place them into his suitcase.

In the evening when she appeared at the restaurant to inquire where he had been all afternoon, he told Madame Papoulias he had been making preparations to leave the next day. She was not surprised; little that had happened in her life encouraged her to expect an agreeable outcome. And then, this professor required endless explanations of even the most obvious things. She only sulked a little because he had not made the arrangements for his flight through her travel agency. "I could have used the commission on the tickets as well as another," she told him.

Following the shore to his apartment that night, Professor Miller wondered at the way the sea left its islands to their own devices. He saw he had traveled too far. For the first time in many months he wished himself back among the good people.

Spies and Lovers

Clyde Hutzler called his home two or three times a day to find out what his wife of thirty years thought of him. In the middle of the day he would recall something he had done that might have irritated Sally. Hearing her voice, distant but friendly, reassured him, often for hours.

Lately Sally had not answered the phone. Clyde knew of no reason for Sally to be out all day. Their son, Donald, was grown and living far away. Sally did not work nor did she care for women's organizations, accusing them of wanting to create a world that was already created.

At the dinner table he said, "I tried to call you this afternoon."

"Did you?"

"Were you out?"

"I suppose so. I wish I could make an enormous *coulibiac* with fresh salmon and a rich dill sauce. Steak and salad every night is *boring.*" Sally prided herself on her gourmet cuisine, but Donald was no longer there to cook for and Clyde was on a diet.

"Are you going out tomorrow?" he asked.

"I don't know."

It seemed to Clyde, who always planned ahead, a suspicious answer. He wondered if Sally's life were being lived elsewhere. Having been brought up to believe that in any situation there were only two possibilities—innocence or guilt—Clyde decided to see what his wife was up to.

The next morning, keeping a discreet distance, he followed Sally's car along the streets of their suburb. Drifts of pink crabapple blossoms leaned lightly against the houses. A number of years before, a service organization had made the trees available at wholesale prices. The residents had planted the whips among their gaslight lamps and diseased elms. The plantings had been a success, although a few residents continued to mourn the dead elms, refusing to take seriously trees with showy flowers.

Clyde had lived in the suburbs all his life. Many of the homes he was passing had been built by his company. People said you could spot a Hutzler house by the quality of the construction—the paneled front door, the built-up roof, the real mullions in the windows.

As he drove along, keeping Sally's car just in sight, he wondered how much longer he would be able to build quality homes. People were not willing to spend the money and good workmen were difficult to find. The painters and plumbers and carpenters who had worked for the company in his father's time had retired. In these last years, Clyde had hired a number of his friends' sons—the friends were lawyers, doctors, businessmen. Their sons said they wanted to work with their hands. They didn't want their fathers' "hassles." They arrived for work with bare chests and cutoffs. The dogs they brought with them made trouble with the neighbors. After they had mastered a trade and would have made good workmen, they quit to become stockbrokers or bankers.

Clyde's own son was in hotel management with a Rockefeller resort in Hawaii. When they had visited the Islands to see him, Clyde had gone to the Honolulu Zoo. In the aviary was a large cage, and in the cage, a single robin. Above the cage was the legend: Robin. This hint that the commonplace might be elevated to the exotic was what he remembered best about Hawaii.

It was hard on Sally, having their son so far away. She wrote long letters fat with enclosures—church bulletins, marriage announcements of Donald's classmates, articles about swimming meets at the Yacht Club, where he had captained the Club's team and where, on summer afternoons, Clyde and Sally had watched him plunge again and again into the blue water of the pool. It made perfect sense to Clyde that Donald should live in a place where it was always summer, but Sally took the distance personally and tried to slip Donald's old world into his new one. Once, before Clyde had talked her out of it, Sally was going to send Donald a deserted hornets' nest they had found attached to their garage. "You know he's always been interested in nature," she pleaded. "It's a work of art. Just look at it. I mean *really* look at it. All those fragile layers, and inside, all the tiny, empty cells, each one exactly the same."

Clyde stopped at the top of a small rise where he could watch Sally, who had parked her car and was crossing the street. Apparently she was going into the library. Once, in a museum, he had been confronted by the original of a frequently reproduced painting; the reality had startled him. He was seeing Sally in the same way; everything about her was at once familiar and new.

She was a large woman, yet her rather heavy body moved gracefully, in an unhurried way that suggested she had all the time in the world. Her hand went, as it often did when she was preoccupied, to the back of her head, where her thick gray-brown hair was drawn into a chignon. Clyde was aware other women no longer wore their hair like that, but he could not imagine Sally's any other way. Her tall, ample figure, a maternal figure, disarmed men. He often saw her at parties sitting on a stairway, or at a kitchen table, deep in conversation with a man who was sometimes a friend, sometimes a stranger. It was clear she was listening to confidences.

"Who were you talking with?" he had once asked.

"Saul or Paul, I think. Something biblical."

"What was he saying?" Clyde had despised himself for having to ask.

"He was telling me what he did. It was something important." She had gazed off into the distance, as though important things by their very nature must elude her.

Sally paused for a moment before entering the library. Because she had no idea she was being watched, she appeared vulnerable. Clyde told himself this must be how a peeping Tom felt; every move the victim made became a command performance. Her defenselessness gave back to him the sense of control he had lost when he began to suspect Sally of being unfaithful. He was alert, watchful of the possibility of being seen, not only by Sally, but by an acquaintance who might wonder why he was parked there. He peered around nervously, but there was no one he knew.

The suburban women had the inessential look of vacationers. Their slacks and sweaters were bright fruity colors—raspberry, lemon, lime.

They wore matching canvas tennies, and peeking over the edges of their heels, like twin rabbit tails, were the white pom-poms of their socklets. One woman carried a tennis racket with a needlepoint cover that read, "This is my racket, what's yours?"

Clyde took in all these details. He had not been this alert since Korea, when he was a point man in a minesweeping detail. He and another man walked twenty meters ahead of the platoon looking for obvious signs—freshly dug earth, a little mound of dried grasses. When they came to a stream, they were the ones to inspect the primitive wooden bridge for explosives. Innocence was the last thing on your mind; it was suspicion that kept you alive. In retrospect that seemed a satisfying time, a time when all of his responses had been heightened.

It was not only the unanswered phone calls that troubled Clyde. Earlier in the week he had come upon Sally in front of a mirror trying on an expensive-looking necklace of jade and gold beads. The moment she saw him, she had snatched it off and dropped it into a dresser drawer, her guilt unmistakable. "Have I seen that before?" he had asked.

"I've had it for ages. You just haven't noticed it."

It was Sally's opinion that he never noticed her. What would she say now, if she could see how intently he was watching as she disappeared into the library?

Clyde did not understand Sally's preoccupation with libraries. When their son was growing up, she had taken him there every week. "We can buy him his own books," Clyde had said, but Sally insisted it was important that a librarian tell the boy to be quiet in the presence of books. Clyde thought that was no answer at all and had told her so.

"I like to watch him take books from the shelves," she had said. "Sometimes when he reaches for a book, I can hardly breathe; the book might change his life."

Clyde thought it ironic that it had been a book about Hawaii, one of those long saga things, that had led their son to look for a position halfway around the world from them.

He sat in the car for nearly an hour. Perhaps she was meeting someone? When he could stand the waiting no longer, he walked up to the library, his heart pounding, and peered into the window of the reading room. It had deep, comfortable chairs and a fireplace, a perfect place for an assignation. Clyde repeated the word "assignation" to himself. He was not sure whether it applied to lovers or spies.

Sally wasn't there. He finally located her in the children's room, hunched up and squeezed into a small chair like an overgrown child, her head bent over a picture book. He hurried to his car.

After she left the library, Clyde followed Sally through heavy traffic to a nearby shopping mall. In order not to lose sight of her car, Clyde had to take chances. He ran a red light and then pulled in front of a large car with a bumper sticker reading, "I Am Driving My Children's Inheritance." He wondered why people were resorting to signs. The car had to brake sharply and the driver gave him a furious look. Under other circumstances Clyde would not have taken such risks; now the risks seemed commonplace, as though cowardice rather than caution had caused him to drive carefully all these years.

He followed Sally into a department store, wondering if the assignation were here, but Sally moved aimlessly from one counter to another. He did not understand purposelessness, especially in Sally, who, in taking care of the house and their son, had been the most organized of women.

It was the middle of the day and the customers were predominantly women. He marveled at their skill in examining clothes on the same rack without getting into one another's way; it was a kind of ballet of small, polite shiftings. Clyde felt conspicuous just standing there and let a saleswoman pull some shirts out of a case for him to examine. During childhood visits to his aunt, the aunt would open a glass-fronted cabinet and take out for him a number of small treasures: souvenir spoons, seashells, a silver thimble, a basket full of foreign coins. The saleswoman, waiting to refold the shirts, seemed to tolerate him in the same way his aunt had, thinking all the while of the cleaning up that would be needed when he left.

Sally went from ties (for some other man?) to shower curtains and then to the housewares department, where she stood watching as a pasta machine was demonstrated. The demonstrator was joking with the women in the audience. "The more you ladies eat pasta, the plumper you get; the plumper you get, the more the boys like you." The slim suburban women smiled tolerantly.

Clyde was cheered by the lively music that came over the loudspeakers. Forgetting for a moment what had brought him there, he told himself it was quite wonderful that he was in a department store in the middle of the day watching long strands of spaghetti ooze from a small machine. He almost never took time off during the week; he would have needed someone to give him permission, and there was no one over him.

Fascinated with the busy machine, he moved closer, until he realized Sally only had to turn around to see him. Hastily he drew back, but not before he felt a little thrill of pleasure in the narrow escape. He saw that if he wished, he might follow her forever and never be discovered. She did not expect him to be there; and so he was *not* there. Somehow the power had shifted back to Sally. To test this theory of invisibility, he edged a little closer to Sally, who was wandering among accessories. She picked up a scarf. It was the yellowish, undecided green of spring leaves. The next moment she was sweeping the scarf into her open purse. The gesture was familiar—one he had seen a thousand times. Whenever Sally found cigarette ashes or a few crumbs on a table she would sweep them quickly into her hand and close her fingers, half embarrassed to be caught tidying up.

Clyde went over what had happened, thinking he might have missed something. Perhaps the scarf had been hers? No. It belonged to the store. He was having difficulty absorbing what he had seen. The music distracted him. It was something by Sigmund Romberg. He remembered how, after a few drinks, his father, who had a fine tenor voice, used to sing "One Alone" from "The Desert Song."

Had Sally been stealing at the other counters when he had been too far away to observe? Clyde believed theft worse than infidelity. You did not go to jail for infidelity. He knew people who were unfaithful and he moved easily among them, while none of his friends were shoplifters.

Sally approached a display of belts. She tried one on, took it off, hung it up, and tried another. Then she tried one and did not take it off, tried a second one, took that one off, and moved leisurely away, the stolen belt around her waist for anyone who cared to see. No one noticed. The saleslady was busy with another customer. The other shoppers were occupied with their own errands.

He was dazzled by her quick, sly movements. He hesitated between judgment and rescue, even escape, yet he could not abandon Sally. He could not stop himself from moving toward her, any more than he could keep quiet when her slip showed or she made a foolish remark at a party; he was the sheepdog hard upon the stray. He put a hand on her shoulder. She swung around. Before she recognized him, he saw on her face a look of exhilaration. She believed she had been caught and welcomed it. Her face was flushed with excitement, an excitement Clyde recognized. It was what he had been feeling all morning, following her. He saw with astonishment that their lives had come together.

A Dwelling Place for Dragons

He chose four fish and placed them side by side so that he might admire their elliptical shape and the delicate yellow of their bellies. The rest of the morning's catch was for the alligator, George. In delivering his sermons over the years, the Reverend Donald Wangeman had made the usual gospel allusions to fishermen. It was not until his retirement to Florida that he had become one. And then it had not been his idea.

His doctor, baffled by the Reverend Wangeman's lack of progress and alarmed that a clergyman should despair, had suggested a hobby. The Reverend Wangeman's wife, Betty, agreed, saying she couldn't clean house properly with her husband underfoot. So each day after breakfast he dutifully set out for the pier with his fishing rod. The rod was one of too many gifts from a congregation whose generosity arose from a bad conscience over having insisted on the Reverend Wangeman's early retirement. He was cast out. That was how he put it to himself. From long association, his simplest thoughts fell into a scriptural mode.

"I'll clean the fish when I get back from feeding George," he said to Betty. He was glad to be through with the day's recreation. For years he had spent mornings in a church office with walls the color of dried leaves and afternoons in the company of the infirm and the grieving. Dazzling sun and sea and svelte, compliant fish should have been a pleasant change, but he could not learn to separate leisure from guilt. He envied his wife, whose housekeeping saved her from vacant moments. He knew that in the back of her mind she carried with her, always, a resource of hidden bits of dust and dirt awaiting her attention.

"You're going to have to stop feeding that animal," Betty warned him, not without sympathy. "Evelyn Ackerman said she'd call the sheriff next time she saw George, and she means it too. She's worried about George eating Bitsy."

"Evelyn Ackerman is a busybody. George wouldn't touch that foul-smelling, yapping poodle of hers." He was immediately ashamed of his harsh words. Mrs. Ackerman was probably as attached to her dog as he was to George and doubtless for a more wholesome reason, but the thought of something happening to George nudged awake a fear that had lain dormant for many blessed weeks.

Ever since his breakdown, when Donald had become for a time quite irrational, Betty had undertaken the task of bringing gently to his attention as much reality as she thought he could stand. Now she said, "Alligators *have* been known to eat dogs. It was a mistake to name George; once you start calling something by a name you're bound to become attached to it. I don't know what you see in that creature. It looks like something out of a medieval bestiary. It's . . . ," she groped for a word, "excessive."

"There's nothing dangerous in an old man having a foible or two," he was pleading, although he knew perfectly well his wife would not be moved by pity where a principle was at stake.

"The sooner you forget about George, the better. There are plenty of other things to do around here besides feeding reptiles. You could start by helping me carry down a load of wash." He had the impression Betty worked at keeping him moving, as though he were a volleyball to be passed rapidly along lest he fall to earth.

In the laundry room they shared with the other residents in their complex, Betty sorted clothes while Donald read the notices taped above the stationary tub. The questers announced their tours for the month: a local air force base, Sanibel for shelling (brownbag lunch), a two-day bus trip to Disneyworld (wheelchairs available). "Mrs. Morgan's having a sale?"

"She's going into a nursing home."

He shook his head. "Her things won't sell. No one has room for them." It was true. Retirees moving south brought with them everything they owned so that in many of the condominiums you had trouble squeezing in and out of the rooms. After all, their history lay in their possessions. "Don't wait lunch." He kissed the top of his wife's head. "I may take a little walk." He had decided on a plan.

The path to the lagoon led Donald through garden patches available to any resident who cared to tend one. Their neighbor's, Mrs. Gutherie's, was full of fleshy roses, flourishing beyond decency in the lush climate and blooming long after you tired of their beauty. Here and there a plot held nothing more than a tangle of weeds and a moldy zinnia or two that had outlived the gardener who planted it.

Beyond their own complex, Donald could see other complexes wrested from the surrounding wilderness of cypress swamp. The condominiums appeared identical, as if mirrors had been clearly placed to reflect, endlessly, one single building. Florida was pocked with these havens, as though a new glacial age were roaring down, sweeping before it the entire population of the north.

The developer of their own complex had seen, in a stream meandering through the swamp, a possible advantage; by damming one of its branches he had created a lagoon, which he then ringed round with ornamental shrubs bearing flowers in florid reds and yellows. The setting gave the appearance of a crudely tinted photograph, but it brought higher rents.

Donald thumped the bank of the lagoon with a large board he kept hidden beneath the drooping branches of a Norfolk pine. Each day while he waited for George to appear, he worried that something might have happened to the alligator—poachers, poisoned meat, the sheriff's patrol. Mrs. Ackerman was not the only one who wanted to do away with George. There were tenants with visiting grandchildren and those who preferred not to know what lounged in the backwaters.

He did not see the alligator approach until George's back parted the water. The landscaped lagoon showed him off to good advantage as an ornate frame sometimes enhances a primitive painting. The blunt snout with its stockade of teeth swung open to receive Donald's fish. When the fish were gone, George sunk slowly beneath the water, not like the sinking of a ship, which is final, but like an orchestra lowered into a pit—the movements below promising future performances.

The alligator's hooded eyes remained above the surface staring at Donald, who returned the look. In this daily exchange, the alligator tacitly acknowledged his true identity to Donald. It was a little joke between the two of them that he should be nurtured by a man of the cloth. For his part, Donald believed as long as he had the alligator eating out of his hand, the rest of the world was safe.

Like many in his profession, Donald had come late in life to the certain knowledge of evil. Though he often spoke of evil from the pulpit, the faces that looked up at him were as against it as he was. Wretchedness, disappointment, suffering were all comfortably familiar to them, but evil was alien, even outlandish. A soldier on the ready, Donald found no enemy to oppose; the battlefield appeared to lie elsewhere, and so little by little he began to disarm. Abandoning the churlish prophets and their endless tales of doom, he spoke only of Paul's charity and John's love.

Then a year ago, a member of his congregation had asked for help for a daughter involved with drugs. "Pastor, I'm ashamed to say this in front of a man like yourself who shouldn't have to hear such things, but she's out on the streets supporting her habit. It's killing me and her mother." The man had covered his face with his hands and sobbed. Donald, in all the years of his ministry, had never put his arm around a parishioner. This was not from any lack of compassion, but because he was afraid the parishioner might flinch. Now he walked over and embraced the man. The daughter had been in one of Donald's confirmation classes. He remembered with regret that he had not succeeded in making her understand the difference between consubstantiation and transubstantiation. Surely, he thought, that had nothing to do with what she had become? He had promised to call on the girl, and upon learning her address, thought she might find his visit less embarrassing if he were casually dressed, but as he walked through the ruinous neighborhood, Donald found himself longing for the protection of clerical clothes. He dismissed his uneasiness, telling himself a man in his calling had a responsibility from time to time to go unprotected. He reproached himself for not knowing that area of the city and considered how he might do a better job of bringing the misfortune of others to his congregation.

It was difficult locating the apartment, for many of the decaying buildings lacked numbers. This anonymity seemed to him the worst part of their neglect. When at last he found the address, he mentioned the girl's name to a young man lounging in the doorway. Because the man wore thick glasses, Donald believed he would be helpful. Looking more closely, Donald saw eyes so full of malevolence, the glasses appeared a protection for others. The man leered knowingly at Donald and pointed to an apartment below street level.

Donald began the descent of a stairway that exhaled the odors of garbage and urine. Its darkness was the darkness of the basement stairway of his childhood and, as then, he had to discipline himself to keep from looking back over his shoulder. He concentrated on what he might say to the girl. His thoughts ran to Mary Magdalene and even to Paul, whose redemption had been so startling. When he knocked at the girl's door, it swung open at once. Donald was shocked to see the girl had dwindled to little more than a wraith: her thin body was a light pencil mark; her hair, clotted strings; her eyes, large and feverish. She didn't recognize him, but she smiled and drew him into the room.

A backpack rested on a chair. Its contents had spilled to the floor and lay in a silky, lighthearted heap. The bed was unmade, the sheets soiled. He thought how shocked Betty would be. On one wall of the basement room someone had painted an orange sun fringed around with rays like a kindergartner's picture. On the opposite wall was the moon with a face drawn on it, but the face was not one a child would draw.

Before Donald could introduce himself, the girl slipped off her light robe and stood naked before him. It was not her corruption that appalled him, but the ineffable longing he felt for her slight body. As he fled, she called after him, "Whatever you want."

The girl began to appear in his dreams. At first she came unbidden, poised and diminutive like the ornament on the hood of an expensive car. Then he found he had only to seek sleep and she was there. This seemed an act of the will and he stopped sleeping.

Shortly after this he had a breakdown, which he did not think of as a breakdown at all, but as a time when everything inside of him was scraped clean, as you would run a spoon around the rind of a melon, scraping away the last bits of flesh. In the months that followed, he had tried to replenish himself and was terrified to learn that, although the Lord made him the first time, this time he was on his own.

Something dark and shapeless filled the emptiness, creeping up into his head and spilling out of his eyes so that his congregation began to avoid him. When Donald gave the Sunday-school lesson, the younger children sometimes cried. Reluctantly, the vestry took over the running of the church and sent him away lest his derangement become contagious.

Darkness settled in Donald's mind like an incubus. Then one day, shortly after their move to Florida, a miracle occurred. He had been looking out over the lagoon when an alligator surfaced, and the sinister presence he had been harboring lifted, gathered itself, and entered the body of the alligator. In his joy and relief he thought of Christ driving the devils into the swine. Donald's only worry was that should something happen to the animal, the devils would be released to reenter the world. Feeling a terrible responsibility, he began to feed the animal so that he might see him each day and be reassured. Mrs. Ackerman's threat to call the sheriff meant Donald must now find a more remote place where his transactions with the alligator could be carried on in secret.

When the alligator surfaced, switched its tail, and began to swim back the way it had come, Donald followed along on the bank. The lagoon narrowed into a stream, and the flowering shrubbery and smooth green lawn became thickets and tangles of sawgrass. The alligator moved through the sluggish water just beneath a dense green mat of water hyacinths. When it surfaced, as a wave rolls occasionally on a still sea, the long scaly body was festooned with a cloak of dainty yellow flowers like an ugly old woman in a girlish dress.

Donald made his way through the tall grass, stepping around the little humps of soft mud, excavated by crawfish, so as not to undo their work. Once he saw a yellow rat snake like a thick coil of hemp, lying indolent and satisfied in the sun. Donald's canvas hat with its jaunty plaid hatband protected his head from the noon sun, but his shirt stuck damply to his arms and back. He told himself he was on a fool's errand and was glad Betty was not there to judge him.

There were gaps in the water hyacinths where he could look down into dark water at the darker shapes of black acara swimming in flighty schools. His shoes were wet and reeked of decaying mud. George led him into a cypress swamp, a shadowed, cool place where the footing was treacherous. Donald had to clamber over fallen trees and watch for springs that oozed up through the spongy ground. There was a sharp, fetid odor which he could not identify. He knew he had only to follow the river to find his way back, yet he felt lost, and worried that he had come too far.

The river petered out into a labyrinth of shallow runnels. The alligator, moving slowly through the muddy broth, was making his way toward a mound of vegetable debris—grasses and sedges. The mound was nearly three feet high and perhaps six to seven feet across. An alligator, somewhat smaller than George, was draped over the dome of the mound like a modeled handle on the cover of a soup tureen. When the alligator saw Donald, it made little guttural noises. A number of what Donald had taken for sticks lying partially submerged in the swamp began to writhe toward the grunting mother. There were too many to count. When he looked for George, he saw the alligator's snout stretched into a wide, paternal grin. Donald trembled. Here in the dark backwaters, George had copulated, and now there were legions of alligators. Donald saw he would never be able to keep track of them all. People must be warned; unwatched, the legions would escape into the world.

Although he retraced his steps, nothing was quite familiar; while his back was turned, the terrain had been subtly transformed. When at last he neared the rows of condominiums, he thought of Betty ascending the stairway, in her arms a neatly folded pile of clean, fresh-smelling linen. He considered what Betty's reaction would be to the warning he brought and foresaw for himself further appointments with the doctor. What if they put him away? Still he hurried on with his message. They had flung Jeremiah into a dungeon but the old man had not ceased his prophesying. He had admonished Babylon, Damascus, Kedar, and Elam. He had warned Hazor it would become a dwelling place for dragons.

Donald stumbled against a shrub. An orange butterfly detached itself and unexpectedly flew at him. Donald ducked out of its way, but the encounter left him shattered and close to tears. It was insupportable that he should be threatened by something so small and delicate. He fell to his knees and waited like Jeremiah for the Lord to deliver him.

Children in the Park

I wore our baby, May, to class. When I raised my arm to write on the board, the straps from the harness that held her to me cut into my shoulders. Her crying drowned out my lectures. Her warmth and light weight were immeasurable.

When I turned from the board, I found my students making faces at May to keep her amused. There were voices in the class that soothed May, and those students I called upon often. Other voices irritated or startled her, sending her into paroxysms of screaming. I discouraged those students from commenting, looking elsewhere when I saw their hands raised. One of them had perceptive, even thoughtful things to say; I missed his comments and he appeared puzzled and hurt when I ignored him.

My students were sympathetic, offering to give May her bottle and not complaining when the bottle warmer blew a fuse, cutting off the classroom lights and nearly losing the students and myself to one another in the dim November morning. But they believed they would be wiser in their planning and cleverer in their arrangements.

We did plan. We did arrange. Duncan and I believed we were not ready for a baby. The word we used was "manage." We believed we couldn't manage a child. We agreed to wait until I had tenure in the university's English department and Duncan had finished his book comparing Engels's theory on the family with Marx's. I like to watch Duncan write. He curls his arm around his paper as though he were sheltering his words. He deals exclusively with facts and is suspicious of my field, which is fiction. "What fiction writers do," he says, "is push all their nightmares off on the reader and then go scampering."

Our marriage is a good one, full of surprises. We have always talked a lot, getting up early and having large breakfasts: waffles, French toast, thin slices of ham, hash browns, country sausage, freshly squeezed orange juice. Duncan worked his way through graduate school as a short-order cook. He cooks deftly and with purpose—as though he were still getting paid for it. We like to sit over cups of coffee and plan how, before anyone else is up, we'll change the world. Duncan wants to switch all the politicians with undertakers. "Undertakers are more dignified," he says, "more circumspect. They're too pessimistic to start a war and they're already used to riding around in big black limousines."

"You'd do better with airline mechanics," I say. "They can handle responsibility and they keep a low profile. They wouldn't start a war either; they'd sit around the oval office in baseball caps and fine-tune and tinker." Even when Duncan and I take long trips together, we come home with a reserve of things we haven't had a chance to talk about.

It was on a trip that I decided, against my better judgment and without consulting Duncan, to have a baby. We had traveled to Mexico for the Christmas holidays, hurrying away from the first skimpy snows. We allowed a day in Mexico City for the Museum of Archaeology in Chapultepec Park, but as stunning as the museum was, after three hours we were discouraged and overwhelmed by the perfect symmetry of the Aztec temples, the Aztecs' clever calendar, the elegant shape of their pots. Selfishly, they had left nothing for us to accomplish. We hurried outdoors, where things were more pleasantly haphazard.

"They had human sacrifices," I said, carping a little.

"Only a few at a time." Duncan is very fair.

It was Sunday and the park was teeming with people. The number of children startled me—at least three or four to a family. The little boys were in short pants and crisply ironed shirts; the girls, in patent-leather pumps, white socks, and party dresses. Many of the youngsters wore headbands from which projected two antennae, each tipped with a pinwheel, so that the children appeared light and buoyant. Adding to this buoyancy were the soap bubbles; the children and many of their parents carried baby-food jars of liquid soap, and the iridescent spheres drifted all around us, kissing us with wet smacks.

At first I was alarmed by the number of children—babies wrapped in rebozos, toddlers taking their first steps, children hanging onto their parents or running on ahead. I felt inundated, smothered by children. I began to photograph them, thinking: series of Mexican children on a Sunday afternoon in Chapultepec Park—something like that. We followed the families through the amusement park and the zoo. I bought more film, greedy for the children, and fed them eagerly into my camera. We were almost out of the park when two things happened. I noticed a small, shabbily dressed girl with no family. She was barefooted, her hair unwashed, her dress too long and hanging in uneven lengths. She had been watching me photograph the carefully dressed children, with no hope of having her own picture taken. The second thing was, I had used all my film.

I beckoned her over and snapped the empty camera. The girl grinned and fled into the park. When she was gone, against my will I found myself crying.

Duncan was alarmed. "She didn't realize you were out of film," he said. He put his arm around me. Nearby, a family had strung balloons from the trees and was celebrating one of its children's birthdays with a huge rococo cake and a bottle of brandy. I knew I was being unreasonable, but I saw myself shuffling hopelessly through the packets of developed pictures.

From Mexico City we went on to one of the old Spanish colonial towns and stayed in a small pension. It was hot during the days but the nights were cool, and in the mornings Duncan would set a fire in our fireplace and we would stay in bed until the room warmed up and the distant mountains, drawing color from the sun, changed from mauve to green. When we got back home, I was pregnant.

I waited to tell Duncan until the doctor confirmed what I knew. Duncan opened a bottle of champagne. "I don't think I should drink," I said.

"If you can't, I won't either." He was pleased to find a sacrifice he could match. I poached oysters in the champagne.

"I've been thinking about the word 'conceive,' " I told him. "It sounds like something you do by yourself."

"That's because you don't know Latin." Duncan kissed the back of my neck as I ladled the oysters, their edges delicately ruffled, onto our plates. "It comes from a word meaning 'to take in.' "

"You're not angry because we're having the baby?" I asked. "It's just that we aren't getting any younger and I thought if we waited we'd be too serious, too worried. I think parents should be spontaneous and impulsive. I think there should be outbursts. And the timing is really perfect. You have your sabbatical this fall. You'll be able to write at home and keep an eye on the baby while I teach."

"I think you have to do more with babies," Duncan said, "than keep an eye on them."

In the beginning everything worked. May was born late in the summer; Duncan's sabbatical began in the fall. We were captivated by the smallness of May's body and the intensity of her needs. I felt a little sad, for never again in her life would she be allowed to be so forthright, so successful in her demands.

Although I was absorbed with May, a part of me longed to be back at the university. In those hours when I nursed May—the warm, damp presence of her body against me like a poultice, her tug at my nipples so primitive, so certain, it needed no thought—I was free to remember my office. I longed for the faded green walls on which I had tacked notices of faculty meetings and postcards from graduated students—students reluctantly released into the world and, like myself, filled with nostalgia for the university. I was forever searching our house for a book, only to realize that at some time or other I had carried it off to my office as though that were where it belonged.

I longed for the students, often in crisis, who flung themselves down and poured out tales of grief—lost loves, warring parents, insupportable professors. Several of the boys had taken to wearing felt hats—fedoras—like those you saw Spencer Tracy and Fred MacMurray wearing in old movies, movies which always ended with a marriage that you knew would last forever. The girls wore waifish, secondhand clothes: men's large, black overcoats with the sleeves folded back, exposing torn linings; men's sweaters with worn patches; men's shirts, the shoulder seams drooping to the elbows. As I listened to their stories of broken homes and separated parents, I saw that they wanted around them their fathers' empty arms.

When fall came I hurried back to the classroom, May weaned and her bassinet rolled into Duncan's study. Duncan was good with the baby. He has large hands into which May fit like a fledgling in a nest. He has a beard he doesn't take seriously; he likes to lean over May and let his beard tickle her stomach. If he has a fault, it is that he is overly conscientious, peering anxiously every few minutes into May's bassinet.

Duncan grew increasingly eager to turn May over to me when I came home from classes, hardly giving me time to shed my jacket and change my shoes. He was anxious to tell me all the things he had done for May. It was a litany with repetitions and an air of sainthood.

"When I get home," I said, "I do all those things too. It didn't occur to me to draw your attention to them."

"Sorry, it's just that I'm not getting any work done on my book. When I do write a paragraph, babies are in it."

"Babies? The book's on Engels and Marx."

"You make them sound like a vaudeville act. I'm writing too much about those sickly babies of Marx's. They were so hungry, they used to bite his wife's nipples until they bled. My book's getting depressing."

"Why didn't Karl get a job?"

"He was writing a book."

"I don't suppose he helped with the children?"

"That was in the 1800s."

"Whatever."

At the end of the second week, Duncan told me he had been asked by the dean to coordinate the students' social-action programs—meetings and demonstrations were accelerating. The students, like bold armchair explorers, were discovering South Africa, Central America, Afghanistan, and the Philippines, the distance of these countries creating among the students an alarming immediacy. "The Dean doesn't want to get into the sixties thing with sit-ins in his office and flag-burnings to turn off the alums."

"We met at a sit-in. You were burning attendance records."

Duncan flushed.

"Why do *you* have to be the one to baby-sit the students instead of your own daughter? You're supposed to be on your sabbatical."

"He *knows* I'm on my sabbatical," Duncan said. "He apologized about that and he'll pay. What he's asking is a compliment. He must have heard how many students came to my Third World lectures. I don't see how I can say no."

"Just say it."

"I can't put my own personal life ahead of these issues." His eyes wandered to the shelves where he kept the Russian dissidents, and I understood he would rather be in the Lubyanka prison facing death than trying to write a book with the baby screaming.

My students were handing in short stories. In the stories there were villains and all the villains were parents—parents who drank, nagged, bullied, deserted, divorced, abandoned, and abused. The students worked on word processors, delivering endless folded and perforated sheets of cleverly written vituperation. In the stories the students took revenge—parents were tortured and shot; there were bloody corpses, fantasized and real. The stories poured in while the parents, miles away, lived in a fool's paradise with no idea that they were spending their last dime so their children could savage them.

Eighteen years from now, what kind of stories would May be writing about Duncan and me? Would she punish us for living our own lives? "Why do the students hate their parents?" I asked Duncan.

"They don't hate them. They're just separating themselves."

"But it's so bloody."

"Tearing flesh from flesh is always bloody."

"Will May separate herself from us like that?"

"I hope so. If not, we're in trouble."

I tried to believe him. Later that week Duncan said, "I told the Dean I'll be available to the students."

"What about being available to May?"

"Why aren't you home by two-thirty? That was our agreement. Your classes are over by two."

It was true. There were days when I lingered in my office an extra hour, hypnotized by the profound quiet and the way the late October sun illuminated my books. I would stand looking out of my office window at the long stretch of grass where on warm fall days the students lay stretched out, their book bags flung carelessly aside, responsibility nothing more than a word.

"I'm sorry, Carol, but it just isn't working out. There must be women who take care of children in their homes?"

Was he implying I wasn't one of them? Many days I went home willingly. May was like one of those novels by Trollope where you know there will be no big surprises, but are satisfied with the ingenuity of the little ones. There was the day when May's eyes, which had been sliding around like two marbles looking for slots, focused on me, and I knew I had become irrevocably a part of her life.

I found Mrs. Craig by word of mouth, which I came to believe meant that no one would admit in writing to knowledge of her. I was hoping for someone matronly—with an apron tied around a generous middle. Instead, a woman not much older than myself answered the door. "I'm Mrs. Craig, but just call me Do." Do's hair was a pink shade of red and she was wearing soiled jeans. She was lean and tough and I thought of all-girl bands and mud wrestlers. Before I could escape with May, she grabbed her out of my arms. May screamed. "You're doing the right thing," Do said. "I can see little June needs socializing."

"May."

The living room was furnished with two enormous lounge chairs oriented toward a blaring television set. The chairs, vacant for the moment, had a lived-in look. On the walls were pictures of startled deer and blazing sunsets painted on black velvet. Duncan and I had agonized over the aesthetic quality of everything that had gone into May's room. We had hung on her walls prints of a Käthe Kollwitz mother and child, a colorful Mondrian, and Dürer's engraving of a rabbit. Exposed to the black velvet monstrosities all day, would May grow up to fancy them? Crowded into one side of the living room were four cribs, three of them with crying babies. "They're talking to one another," Do said. "Isn't that cute? June will fit in real well." A child of about eight or nine was shaking a crib in an overexcited effort to get one of the babies to stop crying. "That's my girl, Jill. She's a great little helper."

A man in jeans and an undershirt wandered down the stairway, "Do, where the hell is my clean shirt? Sorry, didn't know you had company."

I knew I should take May and run, but I had a class in fifteen minutes.

The first week I felt nothing more than anxiety and guilt; panic came the second week when May developed a diaper rash and was ravenously hungry—often too hungry to eat. I told myself she would settle down. When I gave her to Duncan to hold while I made dinner, he said, "She's screaming so much she's vibrating. What do they do to her there?"

"You're not helping my guilt."

"That's not the kind of guilt that needs helping."

"You told me to find a house where I could leave her. You broke our agreement when you stopped taking care of her." After that he didn't say anything. Neither did I. An unstoppable silence grew in the house. We had bowls of cold cereal for breakfast and gave up on saving the world. Even though I needed sleep, the silence was so oppressive, I was glad to hear May's cries in the middle of the night, glad someone had something to say.

I was up with her those deadly hours of three and four in the morning. When I couldn't get back to sleep, I corrected my students' stories. After the brutal and bloody punishments dealt out to them by their vengeful offspring, the humbled parents in the stories were now groveling, confessing the error of their ways—their insensitivity, their selfishness, the irrelevance of their own needs. Sometimes May spit up on the stories so that the papers, when I handed them back to the students, were sour and slightly damp.

I called my mother, who made a principled point of never interfering. "You'll be the best judge of that, dear." I could hear a thousand miles away advice strangling in her throat. She would not tell me to stay home; she would not tell me to stop working; but she managed to give the impression I was living in some country where the language and customs were incomprehensible to her and where, among such oddities, the slightest hint on her part might lead to dangers too obscure even to consider.

I consulted my own childhood. My mother was a seamstress who did alterations in our home. She was terribly proud when my father closed in the breezeway so she could have her own sewing room and an entrance apart from our house for her "ladies." I sometimes wandered in there as a child to look at the neatly arranged rows of colored thread, the button box overflowing with miscellany, a rack of clothes waiting for attention, and another rack of carefully pressed and completed clothes, each one labeled with the name of its owner and the day it had been promised. If my mother was often occupied, she was always home. If I didn't see her, I could hear the humming of her sewing machine. It was the money from the hundreds of lengthenings and shortenings, the takings in and lettings out, that paid my college tuition. "I want you to have a choice," my mother had said.

Each morning as I brought May to Mrs. Craig's house, I met the other mothers. Their faces reflected my haunted look, but not one of us would be the first to speak; we needed Do. On Tuesday Do handed me the wrong baby. On Thursday May's jumper was on backwards. "Jill helped me out," Do said. On Friday the man in the undershirt, who was now wearing a T-shirt that said "Have you hugged your kid today?," was distributing the babies. "Do had to run out for a minute," he apologized.

When I phoned Do to explain that I wouldn't be bringing May back, she was sincerely puzzled. "It's good for babies to have a little fathering," she said. "Wyatt loves kids. He's better with them than I am."

"I believe it," I said and hung up.

I began wearing May to class, smuggling her into the classroom in a book bag, trusting the students not to give me away, but somehow the word got out and Ruth Boyer, the head of my department, called me in. She was dedicated to making things as easy as possible for women, but she wanted to know too much about you. Like those ghouls who sit around a dead body, eating a meal said to contain the dead person's sins, she was nurtured by other people's mistakes.

"How are *things*?" she had asked, her eyes glittering, her voice expectant.

"Things?"

"They must be difficult if you have to take the baby to class."

"It's hell."

"I wonder if there couldn't be another arrangement?"

"The university could ante up for a day-care center." We both smiled at the absurdity of this.

"How does Duncan feel?"

"He's fine."

"I mean about the baby."

"Look," I said, "you want May out of the classroom, I'll get her out."

"Yes, but if there's some difficulty, I might be able to help. I wish you'd tell me just what the situation is. I hope you and Duncan aren't having problems?"

I hurried out of the room.

The next morning when I left for my classes, May was back in Duncan's study.

My classes were pleasant and relaxing. I could call on whomever I pleased, although my back, without May's warmth, felt cold and exposed.

Returning home the second day, I was only a little alarmed to find Duncan's car gone. I imagined May in her car seat beside him, the two of them companionably off on some husbandly errand, perhaps to the hardware store, where you could buy nails and bolts, glues and staples—all those things that fastened together a home.

In our living room a girl, with May draped over her shoulder like an expensive fur, was walking toward me. She looked twenty but was probably older; there was experience in everything she did. She moved lightly, her whole appearance weightless—luminescent skin, pale gray eyes, long crimped hair that floated, a light step moving across my carpet—acknowledging my ownership, but holding onto May. "Valerie Parsons," she said. "We met when the Borders had that party for the grad students." Ralph Border heads Duncan's department. "I guess I should explain what I'm doing in your house." She interrupted her sentences to make little cooing noises at May. "Duncan's my advisor, so he knew I was looking for some work while I finished up my thesis. When he asked me about taking care of May, I was really enthusiastic. I have a lot of younger brothers and sisters—we always had a baby in our house."

May was taking no notice of me. It seemed important to reach for her. It was probably my imagination, but I thought I felt a slight resistance as I pulled May toward me, like silk clinging to silk. I needed to say something pleasant and gracious to this girl. "I'm glad Duncan thought of you. It's exactly what we've needed. You're *sure* you can manage?" I had not been jealous of Do, in whose house May was all mine, but here in my own house, I could see May might make another choice.

"It's no problem. I was really excited to be taking care of Duncan's baby; his Third World seminar was excellent. And of course, I wanted to meet you, too." The girl shook her hair so it fell becomingly around her shoulders.

Duncan's baby. Were Duncan and this wispy girl going to play house in my absence? May was in her dress with the hand smocking, smelling of baby powder and still pink from her bath. "I don't usually put that dress on May; it has to be ironed." It was a small matter but there was nothing else to complain of.

"Oh, no problem. I'll have time to do the baby's wash each day. I love to dress her up. Unless you'd rather I *didn't* put it on May?"

"Is this job going to leave you enough time for your thesis?"

"No problem. I have the afternoons and evenings and Jimmy is good about doing the shopping and cooking."

"Jimmy?"

"The boy I live with."

Evidently she was otherwise occupied and would not take over Duncan—just May. I felt fifty percent better and allowed myself to consider the advantages of the arrangement. Here was someone more experienced than I was. I could imagine her at home—"a lot of younger brothers and sisters," she had said. There would always have been a child at the top of the stairway calling out for clean underwear or vengeance against a sibling. Babies in various states of development would have been handed about. May would delight, but not worry or surprise her. And I could see Valerie was cheerful; that is, she was firmly placed where she was at the moment and did not wish to be somewhere else.

Valerie has worked out. She takes excellent care of May, and seeing the reluctance with which I leave May each morning, Valerie has suggested she keep careful notes for me of everything May does. "No problem. I'm used to taking notes for my thesis," she said. "It's really no different; you make something special out of the ordinary." I wondered if she were making fun of me but her laugh seemed genuine.

If I don't have time to read Valerie's notes in the evening, I take them to my office and there, between the urgent visits of my troubled students, I review Valerie's neat handwriting: "May is cutting two new teeth; May tried to say 'Val'; May ate all of her chopped beans today." I am reading my daughter like a book.

Between classes and the visits of my students, I sit in my office dreaming of our house, of May's room with its toys the color of hard candies, her benign menagerie of stuffed animals, the mobile that hangs over her crib so that she will have no empty moments. I see Valerie and May together. Valerie likes to play a game with May. She covers May's face with a cloth and then whisks it away—appearing and disappearing. This delights May, who squeals with pleasure. I have tried the game with May, but when I play it, May cries.

Sometimes I dream about the children in Chapultepec Park with their headbands, the pinwheels whirring, the children levitating, lifting lightly over the trees and drifting slowly out of sight.

Beneath the Fig Trees

I blame myself. I had no business in that restaurant. The food was blatantly overpriced. I feel the theft and what happened afterward was punishment for my extravagance. When I began grading papers thirty years ago, answers were marked "right" or "wrong" rather than "correct" or "incorrect." It's a subtle difference but it's the kind of thing that leads me to pronounce judgments—especially on myself.

I had come to New York to see my editor about a fifth-grade textbook I was writing. When the rather promising results of my back-to-basics approach had received recognition in the Detroit newspapers, a New York publisher had approached me. With my retirement in the offing, I welcomed a project that would both occupy my time and add to my reduced income.

The offices of the publisher were quite modest; the only amenities, books propped open on dusty bookshelves and plants dying from divided responsibility. The editor and assorted staff were considerably younger than I had imagined them, giving the impression of a house where children answer the door in their parents' absence—their demeanor grave from the weight of unaccustomed authority, but in the background the sound of giggles. It was the giggles that I was afraid of. Because of my age, the staff was deferential. Alone, in an unfamiliar city, I wanted them to be chummy and I began to talk too much. This silenced me, which left us with nothing but the business at hand. There we met on an equal footing, and by the time I left, they were calling me by my first name, which is Alfreda—not a name one uses easily. I resisted an urge to instruct them in how to revive their plants, realizing they had allowed me to retain more of what they called "pedantries" in my book than they would have liked.

After leaving the publishers, I wandered through one exclusive department store after another, searching for modest gifts for my nieces and nephew. I belong to that now extinct breed of unmarried teachers who consider teaching an almost religious vocation. I can see how narrow a view of life that appears these days, almost pathological. But I believe I entered into it innocently and I have few regrets. I still receive notes from students who were in my classes years ago—the very bright ones and the ones who, knowing they weren't bright, guessed at my sorrow for them.

Everything in the stores was too expensive, and I saw I would have to give up the pleasure of seeing my nieces and nephew tear open wrappings with auspicious labels. I remembered *Natural History* magazine in the school library and decided to try the museum gift shop, telling myself education was sounder than luxury. The exploration of the stores had been enjoyable, but I was feeling a growing sense of greed which confused me.

I went into the first little restaurant I came to, eager for at least one hunger to be satisfied. A dozen white marble tables were set in the midst of a forest of fig trees. Fig trees can be seen in all the lobbies and stores in New York. With their constant supply of nervous green leaves they seem to me like the overachievers who are always working ahead of the class. A pleasant young man, obviously gay, with an apron tied around his waist, led me to a table no larger than a dinner plate. There was no room for my purse so I hung it over my chair. I picked up a menu and found avocado sandwiches were nine dollars; chocolate sundaes were five. I considered walking out, but I lacked the courage and told myself New York, like Italy and France, had its own currency.

I ordered a cup of blackberry tea at two dollars and cinnamon toast at three. I assuaged my conscience by thinking of the many things I had enjoyed in the city that had cost me nothing at all. I had timed my trip so I could see the Christmas tree at Rockefeller Center and, of course, the displays in the department store windows: Victorian women in fur-trimmed coats and muffs, skating in Central Park, little girls in white stockings and hairbows and little boys in sailor suits opening presents in turn-of-the-century parlors. The lines of people filing by the windows were clearly enchanted with the old-fashioned tableaux; yet when you look up the word "nostalgia" in the thesaurus, you find it refers to "suffering," "regret," and "melancholy," as well as "desire."

Lately there has been a vogue for movies set in the thirties and forties; the good old days of the Depression and war. Having grown up during the thirties, I can remember what Christmases were in those days. My father, like thousands of other men working in the automobile factories, had lost his job. He had been an engineer in Germany, but in this country he was kept from finding work in his field by a stubborn refusal to learn English. I think he believed it was a waste of time—that so innocent a nation could not last.

He referred to the men on the assembly line with whom he worked as *Schwarzen* and *Schlucker*. Blacks and slobs. Mute, critical, aloof, going off to eat his lunch by himself, a book in a strange language open before him; what must the men on the line have thought of him? When Hitler came to power, they began to call him a Nazi. That wasn't true. He had the greatest contempt for Hitler and wished only that the Kaiser were still on the throne. It was his conviction that people were unable to rule themselves, and it was true that he could not make his life turn out right.

My father gave little in the way of affection to my mother. Her only pleasure came from drawn-out schemes for small purchases. There would be months of looking through shops before she decided on buying a lace-edged handkerchief or a pink chenille bedspread. She used to take me with her to the stores while she visited her projected purchase, monitoring the sales ticket until she felt the decisive markdown had been made. And all the time there was the thrilling danger that someone else might buy it.

When my father lost his job, my mother found work as a housemaid for a family named Davis. At first she was embarrassed to be cleaning another woman's house, but the family made a pet of her. She enjoyed the children calling her name all day long, and Mrs. Davis told her about luncheons and dinners she went to—the menus, the flowers, what the other guests wore. It seemed enough for my mother to be certain those things existed; it was not necessary that she be a part of them, just as you could go for a pleasant drive in the country without owning the land.

My Christmas presents and those of my brother were hand-me-downs from the Davis children, clothes shaped to someone else's body and toys whose secrets had already been explored.

There are people who survived the Depression and who cannot spend enough. Others, like myself, worry over every nickel. Yet as I had wandered through the New York stores that day, I nearly succumbed to alarming temptations. People around me seemed to buy so easily, I felt there must be nothing to it and all my years of caution unnecessary. I, who had never in my life spent more than seventy dollars on a dress, found myself considering a two-hundred-dollar purse, a narrow snakeskin belt with a gold anchor buckle costing ninety dollars, a three-hundred-dollar sweater so soft it rested weightless in my hand.

Sitting at the small marble table sipping my tea, I saw that I had had a narrow escape and resolved to go immediately to the Museum of Natural History, where the glass cases would be full of birds and seasons, things that could not be bought or sold; but when I reached for my purse, it was gone. I looked under the table. I shook out my coat. Had I discovered an arm or leg missing, I could not have been more alarmed. In the schoolroom, I had always kept my purse locked in the bottom drawer of my desk. Shopping that morning, I had clutched it so tightly my fingers had been cramped. What had possessed me to hang it recklessly over my chair? I blamed the fig trees for their disarming air of bucolic innocence.

I remembered a girl in one of those puffy down coats, which I never see without thinking of hundreds of geese having their necks wrung, had squeezed by my table. My impression was of a cloud of crimped blonde hair spilling out of a knitted green cap and a sharp-eyed look I have seen on a child who has found a teacher's weakness. As she brushed against me, she had smiled apologetically.

I had owned the purse for many years and some of the things in it—a needlepoint case for my glasses, a fountain pen, a mother-of-pearl compact—for longer than I could recall. The girl couldn't have been more than twenty-two or twenty-three. She wouldn't even know how a fountain pen was filled. What would she make of my checkbook?

Would the frugal entries arouse her pity so that she would return the purse? Or would she feel contempt? I thought it would be the latter; down coats were expensive.

I had some wild idea of dashing out onto the street to look for her, when I realized I had no money to pay my bill, an unthinkable disaster that made me feel I no longer belonged to the human race. I approached the pleasant waiter, afraid he would think my story a ruse to avoid paying the check.

He couldn't have been nicer. His gray eyes peered sympathetically out at me from under long mascaraed lashes. The few times I tried mascara, I immediately developed telltale smudges under my eyes like the ashes Catholics daub on their foreheads to mark the beginning of Lent. "My dear lady, but that's terrible. You're not to think twice about the bill. I feel so depressed that it had to happen in our place. I'm going to call the police. We've had three purses stolen this week." It was only Tuesday.

The policeman who came wanted to know what was in my purse, but halfway through my inventory, he became restless and interrupted me to assign me a case number: 34361. Did that represent, I wondered, the number of crimes so far that year? That month? That day? The policeman told me I should have put my purse under the table and put my feet on top of it. I apologized for not having known that. I must admit, I was a bit excited at being a part of a New York police report— on the right side, of course. For a moment I felt at the very heart of the city.

Instead of visiting the museum, I had to spend the afternoon notifying my Detroit bank of the stolen checks, calling credit card companies, replacing airline tickets, and getting a small loan from my editor. I expected to be scolded for my carelessness, but everyone was considerate, even a little bored.

The next morning I flew back to Detroit. Any grudge I bore toward New York for what had happened disappeared as the plane banked and the island of Manhattan reared into my window, tilted and shining. Then the city dropped away, and we were over the small towns of Pennsylvania shaped into white crosses by the intersection of snow-covered streets. Drinks were available on the plane, but I didn't have one. I suppose it's a superstition, but years ago I saw a movie with Spencer Tracy in which a pleasure boat burned and sank because the people on it were drinking and gambling. At least that's how I remember it.

Within days my stolen checks began to arrive at the bank. Evidently, the girl was using my credit cards as identification, and the New York stores, in their pleasure at a sale, were accepting them. Each time a check came, I had to go to the bank and sign a statement identifying the check as a forgery. My first reaction to the large amount on the checks was astonishment. I could see the girl in her down coat, floating lightly up and down the aisles of the department stores. The stores would be warmed by the crowds and bright with the pinprick gleam of thousands of Christmas tree lights, the air heavy with the scent of Shalimar and My Sin wafting over from the perfume counters.

I must admit I was envious of the pleasure she would have, moving from one heaped counter to another, ascending escalators, the bounty of the oncoming floor gradually revealing itself, or crowded into an elevator, pressing against the softness of fur coats, and overhead the lighted numbers of the floors to come and the list of what each floor offered. She could have whatever she chose. She had only to write out one of my checks and then disappear into the crowds, carrying with her her heart's desire.

The first check was made out to Bloomingdale's. It was for $315.33. What had she bought? A sweater like the one I had coveted? Instead of dreading the trips to the bank to sign the forgery statements, I found myself curious as to where the next purchase would be made. She shopped at Lord & Taylor, Bergdorf's, Henri Bendel—the names were full of promise. I bought a *New York Times* and studied the ads. Bendel's was especially gratifying; there was nothing in their ad that could be called practical, nothing a person would need. I became excited by the elegance of the things I had come to own. It was, after all, my check and my name that had made each purchase possible.

I began to find my clothes shabby and my apartment uninteresting. Small economies—the habit of a lifetime—seemed to be my life. I thought I might try something more. Browsing in an antique shop, I saw a pair of handsome silver candlesticks and bought them. They cost what had been, before my retirement, a whole week's salary. I'm afraid I was going to pretend they were family heirlooms; it was not only the present I was going to tamper with. That same week I bought a suit of soft, cornflower-blue wool with a real silk blouse. It was on sale, but even so it was a terrible price and the blouse would have to be dry-cleaned. I hurried home with it, and when I opened the box, it broke out of its tissue, vivid as a butterfly emerging from a papery cocoon.

The evening of the day I bought the suit, I was sitting in my living room, taking up the hem, when the New York police called, pronouncing my name in an unfamiliar way. "You lose a wallet with some checks and a couple of bank credit cards?"

"My purse was stolen. The wallet was in it."

"Well, we recovered it. We got your credit cards, and there's still four blank checks remaining."

I had the feeling the policeman was waiting for me to implicate myself. In my mind I had followed the girl willingly, even with excitement and anticipation, up and down the aisles of the stores. But all he said was, "You can have everything back after the inquest."

"The inquest?"

"She OD'd. The coroner said she was a habitual user. That checkbook was a bonanza."

What was he accusing me of? I wanted to tell him I had wished her well. "But if she needed money for drugs, why all those checks from expensive department stores?" For the first time, I felt robbed.

"Jewelry. She bought the jewelry and then fenced it to get money for drugs."

When I took the candlesticks back to the antique store, I received considerably less than I had paid; something to do with the rising or falling dollar, the dealer explained; everything is certainly related to everything else. The suit I wear on special occasions—retirement parties, the Easter performance of Handel's *Messiah* at the cathedral. It is a beautiful suit and it becomes me, but knowing what happened to the girl in the green cap, my complicity makes me uneasy; punishments are even more severe than I expected.

Playing with Shadows

Julia lay still. Movement brought the stab of unwarmed sheet. It was impossible that Mona should have forgotten to turn up the furnace; therefore the furnace must not be working. When Julia had pressed the planning commission in her Sussex village for permission to restore the cottage, the commission had warned of trouble ahead. And so there had been: dry rot, a smoking inglenook, foul drains, and now this. Yet she did not regret squandering the last of her money on the cottage. As time slipped away from her—she would be an unimaginable sixty-one in June—it was steadying to know she had made the ancient walls strong and solid; she could borrow from their strength.

Julia called to the pug, Marcus, to climb in next to her, but he was old now and would not attempt to jump from the floor to the bed. She had just reached down for Marcus and was settling the round animal, warm as a muffin, beside her, when the door opened. Expecting Mona with her morning tea, she pushed Marcus over the edge of the bed. She would not be caught cuddling him.

Instead of Mona in her piecemeal uniform, her gray hair stapled down by black hairpins, and on her face the usual combative expression that dared Julia to find a single thing to tell her to do that she had not already decided for herself must be done, there was Mona, clutching at the door, her hair hanging over her shoulder in a ratty braid and her face white and twisted in an odd way. Mona was wearing one of Giles's old bathrobes, and Julia and Giles had been divorced for twenty years. There was something indecent in this glimpse of a bedraggled Mona.

Although they had shared the single bathroom of the cottage all these years, Julia could not recall seeing Mona anything but fully dressed.

"Oh, Madam," Mona said, staring at the place beside Julia where the dog had rested seconds before, "I don't think I can get down the stairs to make you tea. My arm and leg have gone all needles and pins." An inept puppeteer worked her mouth. Her words had a sliding, unformed sound.

Slurred, Julia thought. She panicked. Mona's had a bloody stroke. Julia saw her day fall to pieces. Her survival depended on routine. She fell asleep each night going over the next day's schedule. Twenty years ago Giles had given her a surprise and she had no need for another.

Mona, who was as invariable as the wrens that lived in the roof thatch, had turned into a capricious actress, abandoning her supporting role for center stage. Julia saw she must deal with Mona's illness. "You're to go directly to bed," she said, anxious to banish the depressing wraith. "I'll call Dr. Welk." As soon as she named her own doctor, Julia had second thoughts. Why should she pay a private practitioner? She could call a National Health man. No, she would not have one of the bastards in her house. Besides, she trusted Dr. Welk. He was not kindly—kindly doctors were liars.

"I don't want to be a bother," Mona was saying, her words sticking to one another like iced cakes. "You had better call Father Burke at the rectory."

A priest! Worse than the National Health. Marcus was prancing around Mona, snuffling at her slippers and nipping the edges of her nightgown. "Leave Mona be," Julia commanded, although she knew Mona was pleased by the attention. "It's nonsense to talk like that," she told Mona. "You're going to be perfectly fine, but do go back to your room and let me get on with things. I don't suppose you turned on the furnace then?"

"No, Madam." Mona gave her a reproachful look and, relinquishing the door as though it were the last handhold on earth, began shuffling awkwardly down the hall, pausing halfway to call back to Julia, "You won't forget Marcus's biscuit? And you had better get your robe on. You wouldn't want to take cold with no one to do for you."

Julia slammed her door against the threat, making more of a noise than she meant to. "Damn," she said aloud, not caring if Mona heard her. She should have gotten rid of Mona, who must surely be in her seventies, long before this, but Julia knew she would not find among the motley crew going into service these days someone who would settle for Mona's wages or who would do Mona's work. The new generation was hopelessly inefficient and insolent as well. Julia paid little attention to these thoughts, which were meant merely to slide over the surface of her fear, to hide it as best she could. When that did not work, she tried optimism. Perhaps it wasn't a stroke at all, but a complication of the neuralgia Mona had complained of for years. Before calling the doctor, who in any event would be making rounds at the hospital at this time of day and would resent an interruption, Julia decided to have her bath and a cup of tea—ritual would save her.

She pulled on her quilted silk robe and walked to the window to see what the weather would be for the golf game she had going that afternoon with Sarah Forbes. April had been warm, and the bridal wreath spilled over the garden wall in a tumble of white froth. The scent from the lilacs and roses beneath her window sent up the various, cloying smells of a perfume counter. Beyond her garden lay green Sussex fields dotted with sheep. Beside the large white dots were smaller dots that were new lambs. She remembered a poem from her childhood:

> The young lambs are bleating in the meadows,
> The young birds are chirping in the nest,
> The young fauns are playing with the shadows,
> The young flowers are blowing toward the west—

Elizabeth Barrett Browning, wasn't it? She could see the worn green book with its faded gold lettering propped up on the nursery shelf. After her mother's death, there had been a procession of nannies, some kind, some cruel, one of whom must have taught the poem to her and her sister, Rowena. No one wrote poetry that stayed in your mind these days. All you saw was gloomy, ugly stuff.

It was a perfect golfing day, but it might be that she would have to remain home and do something for Mona. She couldn't imagine what that something might be. If Mona were really ill, she would get her into a nursing home as quickly as possible. Julia tried to tell herself the prospect of life without Mona would not be entirely unpleasant. Mona was both stubborn and bossy, with an infuriating habit of reminding Julia to do something a moment before Julia did it, so that she was always rushing to get things done before Mona could remind her, and never succeeding because Mona was too quick for her. Julia seldom had the house to herself. Lacking both money and imagination, Mona did not take vacations. The closest either of them came to a respite from one another's company was the sulking that followed their more murderous quarrels, like the clash over whether Marcus was allowed to run free or whether he must be walked on his leash. Julia knew that, left to himself, Marcus would associate with the Hollens's dog, who probably had both fleas and worms and certainly had nasty habits. Mona had insisted that animals had the right to run about and have their little friends. The argument had produced so many days of stiff silence on Mona's part that Julia had finally appeared to give in, keeping the leash hidden away in her pocket on her walks with Marcus until they were out of sight of the cottage.

This morning, with Mona safely in her room, Julia had snapped the leash on the dog before they left the house for their walk. If Mona was spying from her window, let her see. There was a morning freshness about that suggested you were walking through something richer than air. Julia moved briskly along. The gods, deciding someone must become ill, had passed her over and had chosen Mona. It was a bit like a holiday, she thought guiltily. For a moment she felt virtuous, as though she deserved to be passed over, but Mona's pale face floated like a nagging moon in and out of the trees.

She might have walked farther, but Marcus had begun his wheezing and snorting that came now with any exertion. She wondered if she might mention the dog's symptoms to Dr. Welk, perhaps say it was a friend's illness rather than the dog's—but would a friend wheeze and snort? She reached down for the panting dog and, holding him against her breast like a child, carried him back to the cottage, her sense of well-being dwindling.

Julia entered the kitchen where everything was shabby, unfamiliar, and intimidating. This was in contrast to the rest of the cottage, where Mona lavished care on all of Julia's pretty things—handed down from Julia's family or pried from The Yews when Julia and Giles separated. Julia had made the best use she could of Giles's guilt and had been allowed some really quite nice, second-best things: china, rugs, tables and chests, a handsome painting of doubtful provenience—and Mona.

Julia filled the teakettle at the ancient stone sink. The rotting odor of small corpses drifted up from the drain. She noticed the tap leaked badly and remembered Mona wanting the plumber a few years before, but they got a terrible wage and Julia had put her off. The bottom of the kettle was nearly worn through and the wooden handle split down the middle; bits of solidified mineral rattled about in the bottom. She carried the kettle to the cooker, thinking with disgust that the water for her tea each morning came from this poisonous source.

Marcus, recovered now, was standing on his hind legs, front paws scrabbling against the cupboard where the dog biscuits were stored. She made him wait while she got the bread out of its wrapper and put it in the toaster. "Mona spoils you shamefully," she scolded the dog, and then gave him an extra biscuit so he should know his true benefactor. While she was busy with the biscuits the toast burned, and she hurried to open the window so Mona would not know. The toaster was a hazard, spitting sparks when it was plugged in. Why hadn't Mona told her? Perhaps she had. Should she take some tea up to Mona? But she had not boiled enough water for two cups. Better wait and see what the doctor said. She hurried from the kitchen as from the scene of a crime, carrying her cup into the drawing room, and settled next to the phone. The nurse, Miss Bricker, in promising to pass Julia's message on to Dr. Welk, managed to convey that a house visit would be a very great favor. Bitch, Julia thought, and slammed down the receiver.

It would be nice to have a fire going when the doctor came. Mona would have had one lit by now. Julia had seen Mona set the fire a thousand times, but she could not recall exactly what must be done. With the help of yesterday's *Times* and some paraffin, she managed to get a blaze going. She had met the doctor, and his rather dim wife, at the golf club. He was not unattractive, with his formal manner and perpetual frown, and she regretted he was not coming at the end of the day when she might offer him a drink, liking the idea of the two of them sitting companionably in front of the fire, chatting about Mona behind her back.

She was congratulating herself over building the fire when drifts of smoke began billowing into the room. She had forgotten to open the flue. She ran into the kitchen for the kettle and, after dousing the fire, watched horrified as black, ashy water seeped out toward her Chinese rug. "Bloody hell!"

The rug yanked out of the way, she sank into a chair, telling herself she must stop all the mad activity. She had had her bath, dressed, walked the dog, fixed tea, and called Dr. Welk. Nothing more need be expected of her. As she sipped her tea, cold now, she looked around the room for comfort. Just now, in the States, the English country look was very popular, but of course it could not be achieved where people had to buy their things. She took pleasure in the celadon green Fortuny drapes at the terrace windows, the little boxwood escritoire, the hunt table, and the painting that might be by Stubbs, of a white stallion with its arched neck and wild eye. She especially liked the painting for its suggestion that you were tamed at your own pleasure. Those things had all come from The Yews. Julia had kept most of the wedding gifts as well; even after forty years she could not look at them without seeing in a crystal decanter or a silver candlestick a reflection of the giver's face. It was depressing to think most of them were gone now.

The library steps and a Chippendale chair were from her father's library. It was ironic that they had come to her, for as a child she had not been allowed by her father into the room. After her mother's death, her father had become more and more of a recluse, shutting himself away each evening, regarding his small daughters, on the rare occasion when he came upon them, with a look of perpetual surprise.

Hard up as Julia was for money these days with this tax and that, it never occurred to her that anything might be sold; it would be like stealing from herself. Her things were to go to her son, who was in Rhodesia. She would not use the country's wog name, not even when Robin got after her about it, warning her the letters she sent might not be delivered. One of these days things would blow up down there and Robin would come home. He had been married twice and was single again; Giles had set him a poor example. She had tried to make friends with each of Robin's wives, but like most girls these days, they had been too long in school. They were thin, dry little things with an opinion on everything, always lugging books about and showing off what they read in high, urgent voices; so much alike she couldn't think why he had traded one for the other.

Julia heard a noise overhead. Good Lord, what a sod she was, forgetting about Mona. She hurried up the stairs to find Mona bent over the tub.

"I came in to tidy myself for the doctor and saw you'd had your bath, Madam. I couldn't leave a mess for the doctor to see when he comes in to wash his hands."

Julia was furious. Mona never stopped complaining of the bath oil she used because it left a greasy ring. It was like her to take this opportunity to drive the point home. Still, she was relieved to see the job done and just in time. She heard Marcus barking at the sound of the doctor's car in the driveway.

"T. I. A.," Welk said, "transient ischemic attack." Doctors never spoke English. Of course he had suggested "hospital," and just as predictably Mona had refused, making such a scene that to quiet her Welk gave in.

Julia stood with the doctor at the bottom of the stairway, speaking in low tones so Mona could not hear. "Just how serious is it?" she asked, trying to keep her voice steady.

"From your description of her appearance this morning, there has been improvement already. Wouldn't be surprised if her symptoms were gone by tomorrow; the recovery in these cases can be quite dramatic."

Julia felt an angry joy. It was possible her own life would go on as it always had—she need only get through a few days of inconvenience. At the same time she was irritated. All this fuss, and Mona wasn't to die or anything like it.

"That doesn't mean there couldn't be a second, more serious episode," Welk warned. "You'll want to keep her quiet for a bit." Marcus was snuffing at the doctor's crotch, and Julia gave the dog a kick. "I know it's not quite your line," she said, "but the dog wheezes and coughs when you walk him."

"Might be heart," the doctor said, and added rather pointedly, "I've heard good things about the new vet in Boxly." He inquired after Julia's golf game and promised to return the next day to check on Mona.

"That's kind," Julia said. "Miss Bricker was rather a bear about your coming." She added brightly, "Stop by on your way home and you can have a drink to wind down."

"Thank you, but I never touch the stuff during the week. If it's convenient, I'll be back the same time tomorrow."

Julia felt the snub, and when the door had closed behind the doctor, she marched upstairs to take it out on Mona, alarmed at how upset Mona's illness had made her, for, since Giles had left her, she had had no wish to rely on someone again. "You made a proper fool of yourself with Dr. Welk," she accused Mona.

Mona appeared contrite. "I didn't want to make a fuss, Madam, but a hospital is no place to be when you're sick. You don't want strangers about at a time like that." Marcus had managed to leap onto Mona's bed and was pushing the blankets about with his muzzle to make a nest.

Julia resented the dog's sudden agility. "Well," she told Mona, "I can't afford to get someone in to take care of you." It was true. This year, for the second time, she had inched into capital.

"I'm not long for this world," Mona said, testing what the doctor might have confided to Julia. "There's no need to waste your money on me, Madam."

"That's absolute nonsense. Dr. Welk said if you do as you're told, you will be perfectly fine in a few days. Remember, you're not to get out of bed." She rather liked giving Mona orders. Her bossy tone was modeled on Mrs. Dort-Grieves, who had been headmistress at her school and whom she had not thought of in years. She could barely recall her school years. Her set didn't go in for books. Even Mona read more than she did, sneaking the *Times* after Julia had culled the death notices and the court calendar.

Julia eyed Mona, deciding she must do whatever one did for sick people so they got better and ceased being a nuisance. "I'm going to fix you tea and toast and an egg."

"Oh, Madam, you've never cooked an egg."

"Not true," she said triumphantly. "At school we used to cook plovers' eggs over a candle in our rooms. Remember, if you get out of bed again, I'll send you directly to the hospital." In her new headmistress role, Julia looked quickly about. She could not remember the last time she had been in Mona's room. Her restraint was not from any scruple— she simply had no curiosity about Mona. She was surprised to find the room had taken on a life of its own, that it was not just a servant's room but appeared to exist quite apart from Julia's own taste. There were grotesque religious prints tacked to the walls—a heart dripping blood and an effeminate Christ. A show of one's religion was distasteful to Julia, who attended the local Church of England at Easter and on the occasional late winter Sunday when dark skies and bare earth had a mysteriously pious effect upon her.

She saw Mona's bedspread, neatly turned back, was not the plain white cotton one she had purchased years ago for Mona, but a fuzzy thing in a hideous pink color. On the dresser were a number of framed snapshots. As far as she knew, Mona had no close family. Yet the faces stared out at Julia, trying to catch her attention. On the bedside table was a little horror of a lamp—an indeterminate and unbearably coy china animal with a ruffled shade perched on its head. It had not occurred to Julia that Mona would want to read at night, and so she had never thought of a lamp. The books on the table were thin, ugly, black things, probably devotional; it appeared Mona had her own needs. Julia began to feel less a headmistress and more a trespasser. "I'm going to cancel my golf game," she snapped and, tugging at Marcus's collar to dislodge him from the bed where he lay with his chin on Mona's leg, hurried the dog downstairs.

She managed rather well with the egg and the toast, only having to spoon away a bit of slimy white in the slightly undercooked egg. As she passed the terrace door, the lilacs caught her eye. She went into the garden and broke off one of the double-white ones, self-consciously placing it on the tray. It was an act that astonished her, for she would as soon run naked into the street as do a sentimental thing.

Mona appeared to be dozing, her head positioned like a centerpiece in the middle of the pillow, her hands crossed over one another outside the sheet, a rosary tangled in her fingers. When Julia saw the sepulchral pose, she knew at once Mona was trying to intimidate her. She walked noisily into the room and Mona's eyes snapped open. The lilac caught her eye and she reached for it. "It's one of the ones you planted when we first moved in—Joan of Arc or some such," she said in her muffled speech.

How on earth did she know that, much less remember it? Was there anything about her Mona did not know? It was damned eerie. Julia saw that should something happen to Mona, the last person on earth who understood her would be lost, but perhaps that would be best.

"I was having the strangest dream, Madam. I was trying to climb the stairs to my room up on the fourth floor at The Yews. It used to get the morning sun, not dark like this one. The stairs seemed to go on forever and I couldn't get to the top of them, but the climbing in the dream must have done me good; the needles and pins are gone."

Julia asked a question which, strangely enough, had never before occurred to her. "Why did you leave The Yews and come with me after the divorce instead of staying with Giles?"

Mona's face, which had been flaccid, as though it lacked bones to shore it up, now took on its familiar shape. She appeared relieved to be asked the question; she might have been waiting for many years to give an answer. "You were the stronger one of the two, Madam." One corner of her pale mouth wormed into a sly smile. "The other servants couldn't see it. They thought they had a future with Master Giles, but I knew how it would go. It was your temper, Madam. When I saw you throw the bowl of soup at Master Giles, I knew you were a fighter."

Julia was pleased with the first compliment she had ever received from Mona. It was true. She had outlasted Giles, who had been dead for six years. The Yews was stripped of its pictures and furnishings now, even the library *boiserie* had been ripped out. His second wife had to resume her law practice. Julia told herself, poor as she was, she did not have to slave away in some office. Secretly she envied the woman who had been admitted to a man's world, which Julia long ago had decided was the only world there was.

She reconsidered Mona's remark. Wasn't there something ominous in it? Had Mona looked after her all these years, believing the day would come when Julia must care for *her*? The responsibility was unwelcome, was all wrong; Mona was paid to take care of Julia, and Julia would not see the world slip around to anything else.

She walked over to the bed to collect the tray. Mona, who had always seemed a large presence, appeared small, shrunken, a rag doll. Julia felt a sudden pity and beyond the pity, panic. She fussed awkwardly with Mona's pillow. Julia thought there must be something wrong with her; so much had slipped out of her hands—Giles, whom she had truly cared for, and her sister, Rowena. The doctor had warned her that Mona might have another stroke, and Marcus was getting weaker each day. It appeared she was the only one with a talent for lasting. But she did not want to be the last one left. You could overdo survival.

"You look rattled, Madam. You're no good to me here, tugging at my pillow. Let me be and go into the garden. It will settle you."

Julia was relieved to be ordered from the room, which depressed her; the ordering itself was reassuring. Mona was right about the garden. It always did Julia good. At The Yews, Julia had never dirtied her hands. There had been a staff of gardeners to do her bidding, but here there was no one but herself. When they had first moved into the cottage, the grass had been a tangle and the flowers florid and ugly as cheap china plates. An old hand mower lay in the toolshed, but there was no money to hire someone to use it. She had dropped some hints to Mona, but Mona had been quick to say, "My back would never allow it, Madam."

Julia had dragged the mower from the shed and had started to push. The neat swaths of stubble had been rewarding, and the smell of new-cut grass heady. Back and forth, back and forth she had gone, the exertion unique and strangely calming. When the job was finished, she had come in to tea to find freshly baked gingerbread, Mona's unspoken and rare approval.

Now Julia brought out some secateurs and began hacking away at the overgrown shrubbery. The sharp twigs slapped her, and there were briars with nasty thorns. This was like the world she had been living in, and she was glad for revenge. She remembered how she had torn out the world she had been living in, and she was enjoying the way the earth gave way to her trowel and then allowed itself to be gathered in again and patted firm about roots that only moments before lay bare and vulnerable and near to death.

Today she was glad to escape the stale closeness of the sickroom. In contrast to what was going on in Mona's room, everything in the spring garden was commencing, suggesting to Julia there might yet be other lives to live. She tried some of these lives out: her son sent for her to come to Rhodesia and live with him in a house with many obliging servants who slipped quietly about, cheerfully doing her bidding; the doctor's wife died a quick, painless death, and after playing several games of golf with Julia, the doctor, now without his frown, proposed; the painting turned out to be a genuine Stubbs, and with the money it brought, she leased the land that separated her cottage from that of the Hollens's, raising a fence to keep the Hollens's dog away from Marcus and planting a winter garden with Christmas roses and snowdrops, witchhazel and early dogwoods and the heather that had gold flowers in winter. She would never have to suffer bare earth again, but any day of the year might walk outside and find something blooming. Against Julia's will, Mona appeared in the background, ordering about the servants in her son's home, serving the doctor his breakfast, lifting Marcus over the fence and into the Hollens's yard.

At noon Julia heated a tin of chicken broth for Mona, adding to the tray a little snack of crackers and a bunch of grapes. She was starved after her work in the garden. The lunch looked so attractive, she was tempted to sit down at the table and eat it herself.

Mona peered at the tray. "You oughtn't to have gone to so much trouble, Madam." Marcus was lying just inside the door. "He came up all by himself," Mona said triumphantly. "He misses his old Mona." She tasted the broth. "I don't suppose you brought the salt and pepper?"

Julia, who had been waiting for praise, stamped down the stairs. When she returned, she saw Mona had finished the broth.

"I didn't want the soup to get cold," Mona explained.

Julia, tired from the climb, sank into a chair, a useless shaker in either hand. Mona always got the better of her. It was because she knew Julia so well, while Julia knew her not at all. "Who are the people in the snapshots?" she asked Mona. Perhaps it was not too late to make some discoveries of her own.

"The woman standing in front of the house is my sister in Canada. The girl in the round frame is my niece, Doreen. She has her own hairdressing shop in Toronto. The young man in the glasses is my nephew, Father Ed. He's a Jesuit. It takes ever so long. I asked him to remember you in his masses when you had the surgery for your piles."

My God, Julia thought furiously, that smug-looking man praying over my backside. "Well," she said nastily, "we'll have to get word to him about *you.*"

"Oh, Madam," Mona smiled indulgently at Julia's ignorance. "I couldn't ask for *myself.*"

Julia looked suspiciously at the small black books. Was it possible that all these years Mona had been praying for her? It was an infuriating thought—lumpy cupids flying about unseen just over her head, influencing her in ways she might not like. It was very unfair of Mona.

"If I should be taken, Madam, you'll send my things off to my sister?"

Julia wondered what Mona possibly had to give. Did she expect Julia to pack up the tacky bedspread and the thin black books? Where *were* Mona's things? Julia knew perfectly well. They were all over the house—the Fortuny drapes Mona brushed spring and fall, the little boxwood escritoire she rubbed down once a month, the silver candlesticks she polished—even Marcus, whom she fed and petted and had all to herself when Julia was out. More than Julia, Mona owned Julia's things, knew their little secrets. For a moment Julia had the wild thought that the entire contents of the cottage would have to be packed up and shipped to the goose-faced woman in the photograph so that the woman might continue with Mona's brushing and polishing.

"And Madam, there's something I want you to have."

Julia was irritated. Was the grotesque lamp to be thrust upon her to glow ominously in the dark like Mona's disembodied soul? She did not want to talk about something happening to Mona.

Mona was fumbling with the drawer at her bedside table. She unwrapped a yellowing linen handkerchief. Sheltered in its many foldings was the small, gold circlet Julia had seen Mona wear each Sunday on her way to church. "You needn't be ashamed of it," Mona said, "It's real gold. I know you wouldn't have something that wasn't quality."

Julia was unpleasantly reminded of an aunt who, years before, during some trifling illness, coaxed sympathy by promising Julia an ugly sapphire brooch, and Rowena, Julia's sister, the much more desirable pearls that had been in the family for ages. Rowena's daughter had the pearls now. The brooch had been sold. Julia had often thought she would like to have a daughter, someone to call up and gossip with or to go up to town and meet for lunch at the Buttery at Fortnum's. Someone you might take to N. Peal for a cashmere sweater or AnnaBelinda for one of those Victorian lace blouses that were so fashionable now. Then, if you were ill, as Mona was, the daughter would come round and look after you, and when you were gone, she would take proper care of your things. Julia worried about her things, for how could she possibly ship them halfway around the world to her bachelor son in Salisbury, where unquestionably there were termites and wood worm?

Mona had no daughter either, and was now telling Julia the one valuable thing she owned was to go to her. And what did that mean? Julia was alarmed at the pleasure she felt. "This is nonsense, Mona. You're going to be perfectly well." Julia despised soppy scenes. "I've a great deal to attend to; this house doesn't run itself." Importantly, she stood up, but could think of nothing to do.

Mona saw the hesitation and understood at once. "You'll want to order something for supper," she said with satisfaction at Julia's uncertainty. "We finished the lamb last night. You could get some tinned salmon, and the tomatoes are beginning to come in. There'd be no cooking then. And a little bit of meat for Marcus. Anything fat gives him bloat."

After calling in the order—veal chops which the butcher told her how to prepare—Julia canceled her golf game. "It's a terrible bore, but Mona has gotten herself sick," she told Sarah, as if it were a deliberate act on Mona's part.

Julia hung up the phone and found herself adrift in the silent house. Marcus lay sleeping on his back, his feet up in the air like an overturned beetle. Rain had come, locking her out of the garden. She listened for sounds from Mona's bedroom and, alarmed by the silence, climbed the stairs and put her ear to Mona's door until she heard the little steam whistles of Mona's breathing.

Downstairs again, she wandered from room to room like a museum visitor, letting her hand rest on a chair or a table, which felt lifeless under her touch. Once she had believed she would like to be buried as the Egyptian pharaohs were, with her possessions about her; now she saw they would be no comfort. It occurred to her that some of them might be sold. Even with all the bloody taxes, it would give her and Mona enough to hire a drudge to come in once a week and take the heavy cleaning off Mona's hands. She might even take Mona to the sea to recuperate. Julia tried to imagine the two of them sitting together on the porch of a hotel looking out toward the sea, saying what?

When the groceries arrived she examined the two chops, finding them a sickly color and remarkably inert. She tried to recall what the butcher had said must be done to render them edible. Perhaps she

ought to make some sauce to accompany them? Something a rich
brown, laced with wine, to liven the veal up, but she did not know the
first thing about making sauces. She had no skills. She played a little
golf, some indifferent bridge, and gardened; time killers that any fool
might learn.

She put the chops on. They looked companionable nestled one
against the other. Tired of her own company, she poured out two sher-
ries and, making plenty of noise so Mona should be awake, mounted
the stairway.

Mona was sitting up in bed, her hair combed and color in her
cheeks. "I thought we'd have a drink while the chops are cooking,"
Julia said, enjoying Mona's shocked look at the mention of the chops—
or was it the idea of having a drink with Julia? Whatever it was,
it was something Mona had not been able to predict. A small triumph
for Julia.

"I don't think there's another bottle of sherry when that one's gone,"
Mona warned. Julia was amazed to hear Mona's words had regained
their beginnings and ends. Something that might be hope nudged her.
She held the glass out to Mona, who took it gingerly as though it might
writhe in her hand.

"Never mind," Julia told her. "There's going to be money for more
than sherry." She was relieved that Mona was recovering, but she did
not mean things to go back to the way they were. Julia meant to stay in
charge. "I've made some plans for us."

"Oh, Madam," Mona said, her voice oily with pleasure, "I can
smell the chops burning." She took a long sip of her sherry and the two
spots of color on her cheeks brightened.

Julia rushed downstairs, swearing, grateful for the petty quarreling,
which was something you could not do by yourself. The chops were
salvageable. Marcus, who had followed her, first up and then down the
stairway, lay stretched out on the kitchen floor panting. Julia poured
herself the rest of the sherry and sat down beside the dog while he got
his breath back. She stroked the familiar coat. If something happened
to Marcus, she wondered, who would carry back and forth between
Mona and herself, like an old, dry bone, their love for one another?

Sympathy Notes

I first noticed the tent in early fall, about the time Mrs. Murchis received a note from the family of Henry Fonda acknowledging her letter of condolence. A fog from Cook Inlet had rolled over Anchorage. As it met the cold pavement, the mist turned to ice, forcing morning traffic to a crawl and leaving plenty of time to look around. The tent was orange and dome-shaped, a second sun pushing up through the pine trees. It was like the one Wade and I had given our son, Jay, for his eighteenth birthday. I thought, without much hope, Jay had come to take me home. I did not believe I could get through another Alaskan winter and even if I could, when it ended, Larry and I might not be together. He was tired of my punishing him for the cold and darkness, which he hardly noticed and which was not his fault.

The tent was in a small park I pass on my way to the library where I work. Although I told myself it could be anyone's son, that thousands of people come to Alaska eager for the wilderness or the lack of civilization, I looked expectantly each day for some sign of the occupant. The end of the second week I saw a figure piling wood beside the tent. It was not Jay.

The library is in the small village where Larry and I live. The village, more outpost than suburb, is about twenty minutes beyond Anchorage in the foothills of the Talkeetna Mountains. We have a lot of timber hippies living here in shacks left behind by prospectors. They are like beautiful horses with their long manes and skittish ways, nibbling on grains. They come into the library and take out books on drying food and midwifery. There are fundamentalists here too, who keep an eye on our bookshelves for salacious literature. Their children, who are optimistic and courteous, check out catalogues for Bob Jones and Oral Roberts Universities. The fundamentalists have their own local radio station, and driving to work, I sometimes hear them asking of their listeners impossible things.

Mrs. Murchis comes to the library nearly every day, looking up addresses in *Who's Who*. When John Wayne died, she sent a note of condolence to his wife and and in return received a handwritten reply. Since then she has made a practice of writing to the families of famous people who have suffered a loss. She tells me she often stays up late into the night searching the Bible for a comforting phrase. Her pride and joy is a card, bordered in black, bearing the royal crest of the Grimaldi family. The solemnity of the envelope, also bordered in black, is broken by one of Monaco's brightly colored stamps. Mrs. Murchis has received invitations to speak to local organizations about her hobby and to exhibit her scrapbooks, which are filled with acknowledgments from the grieving families of stricken celebrities. The deaths of these strangers have changed her life.

The first frost came early this year. The leaves fell off the trees suddenly and with much effort, shoving the distant mountains closer like a mother giving a push to a reluctant child. In the park, a light dusting of snow lay on the orange tent. A thin glaze of ice would form over the tent flap in the mornings. Each new day would begin for the owner of the tent with the breaking of a seal.

The afternoon of the first fall storm, the boy in the tent appeared at our library. Bess Truman had died the day before and as he walked in, I was on the phone giving Mrs. Murchis Margaret Truman's address. Mrs. Murchis was apologetic. "I would have come in myself, Liz, but the man who shovels my driveway hasn't turned up yet." Larry had been out at six clearing our driveway. He regards the Alaskan winters as a challenge. He comes in from chopping wood or shoveling snow to collapse happily into a chair and say, "This beats being a CPA in the big city." He is still a CPA, but instead of filling out tax forms for lawyers and doctors, he works for the native tribes. Because of the pipeline, many of the Indians and Eskimos in Alaska are wealthy, but they regard the modern office buildings and hotels that have been erected with their money as a kind of conjuring trick, less real than the specters that appeared to their forebears as they walked across the endless and empty miles of ice.

Like my son, Jay, the boy was in his early twenties, but Jay is dark, average height, and rather compact—he holds down any room he walks into. This boy was slim and rangy, with narrow shoulders and thin, bony wrists. His unexpectedly lavish red beard was grizzled with snow. He might have been a Scottish chieftain leading ragged troops over Ben Nevis or Barbarossa tramping across the Alps. Obviously well brought up, he stood on the mat inside the doorway carefully brushing off his jacket and stamping the snow from his boots. The table he chose was on the opposite side of the room from my desk. He extracted a jumble of papers, arranged like a clumsily put together pack of cards, and spread them out in front of him. As he warmed up, he shed his jacket and down vest. His clothes were L. L. Bean or Eddie Bauer, the kinds of things we used to give Jay for Christmases and birthdays. Jay has left law school and is in Texas now, working on the oil rigs. He has let us know he has no further need for our gifts.

It was not surprising that the boy would come to the library for comfort. His mother would have taken him to a library, as I took Jay when he was six, so that he might have his own card. Later he would have walked over from school with his class to learn about the *Readers' Guide* and the card catalogue. " 'Let's have the little red-haired boy in the back row tell us what he's interested in. The stars? We'll pull out the drawer that says AM to AY. Now step up here in front.' " We librarians, who give the impression that everything can be known, have much to answer for.

When I left my husband and son and came with Larry to Alaska, the first summer was all I had hoped it would be. We found a small house with a view of the mountains and a new wood stove. We decorated it with Eskimo carvings and Indian prints. We went hiking in the mountains. I froze berries and Larry caught salmon. We congratulated ourselves for staying away from the sons and daughters of Philadelphia lawyers and New York stockbrokers, who build contemporary homes in the expensive Anchorage suburbs and furnish them with family heirlooms—Chinese-export punchbowls with hairline cracks and threadbare Oriental rugs. They fly to San Francisco in the fall for clothes and Hawaii in the winter for vacations and subscribe to the

Sunday *New York Times,* which arrives in the middle of the week, giving the soothing impression it is just a little too late to do anything about the problems of the world.

From the beginning, Larry loved Alaska, while I kept feeling I had forgotten something. When the winter came I stayed home, making innumerable cups of tea and writing long letters to Jay explaining why I had left his father. There were spectacular things to see—one morning the hoarfrost bunched on all the tree branches like thousands of crystal knives. By February I was visiting the supermarket every day for the bright colors of the fruits and vegetables flown up from California like planeloads of tourists improbably dressed for summer.

I would call Larry in the late afternoon and suggest meeting at the Captain Cook Hotel for a drink. Sitting in the elegant lounge, it was possible to imagine I was back in the city we had left. But when we walked out of the lounge, there would be the stuffed bear in the lobby and, only a block or two from the modern buildings on the main street—log cabins and stores with wooden fronts selling prospecting supplies. When Larry told me I ought to find something to do, I remembered Simone de Beauvoir had said, "Books saved my life." I applied for a job here at our local library, which is nothing more than a storefront. My master's degree in communications won out over someone with a Ph.D. in farm management.

The boy came to the library every day. I discovered his name was Eric. After he warmed up, he would disappear into our restroom for a bath. I could tell what he was doing from the water all over the floor. It was hard to imagine his tall frame cracked into grasshopper bends as he lifted his feet to the washbowl. The bath took several minutes. If no one else happened to be in the library, this gave me a chance to look through his things. Even without his permission, I was anxious to know the boy and curious about the way he would write furiously for an hour at a time and then sit idly, staring out the window at the distant mountains as if the right words might come trooping over the snow-covered peaks.

I found a budget among his things with alarmingly little allotted for food. There was also a package of unopened letters from a woman in La Jolla. He was working on a novel, and I was startled to find it was my life. The son in the novel could have been my son; the man might

have been the man who had been my husband; the suburb, the one I
had left so eagerly a year and a half before and whose tame streets were
constantly on my mind like an errand you are trying not to forget.

Eric described homes that were French provincial châteaus or Geor-
gian colonials, a yacht club modeled after a Venetian palazzo, an early
American high school. He rather heavy-handedly contrasted this sam-
pler of western civilization with the falling apart of families—of one
particular family. I read hungrily about cocktail parties, needlepoint
and gourmet shops, stylish clothes. It was exactly what Larry and I had
wanted to escape. I now found their description so strangely exciting, I
was upset by Eric's dismissiveness. He must have had some pleasant
memories—working on his car in the driveway on summer afternoons;
long-legged girls in their tennis dresses stopping by on their way to the
club; coming home late on a summer night when the bulky shadows of
trees fell across the road and people were asleep in their homes and he
had all the streets for himself.

If Eric noticed that someone had gone through his papers he gave no
indication, but continued to stare out at the mountains. Midwesterners
consider mountains an aberration and are always waiting, even hoping,
for them to disappear so everything can get back to normal.

Early in November Brezhnev died, and Mrs. Murchis came to the
library to copy out the official title of the Soviet Union. It excited her to
write to a Communist country, but she worried about being disloyal.
That same week a moose ate the azalea bushes I had planted at the side
of our house; our pipes froze, flooding our kitchen; and Larry, who
had begun flying lessons as soon as we had arrived in Alaska, bought a
quarter-interest in a plane and began flying up to Kotzebue and
Tanunak and Kwigillingok on business. I had thought we were coming
to Alaska so that in the midst of emptiness we would stay close to one
another; instead, Larry was gone several days each month to places in
which I could not believe. To keep myself from merging with the
emptiness, which seemed all around me when Larry was gone, or
thinking too much about Jay, I sometimes spent the evenings wandering
through a large shopping mall which might, except for the usual stuffed
bear, have been a shopping mall anywhere.

Sometimes I went to a movie, particularly if it were about a large
city. One evening on my way to see a Woody Allen film at the univer-

sity, I stopped in at the student cafeteria for dinner. It is a handsome room with a fireplace and a reflecting pool surrounded by greenery and windows three stories high looking out on the Chugach Mountains. Eric was sitting alone at a table. Remembering his skimpy budget, I filled my tray with more than I could eat and headed in his direction. He immediately got up and hurried away leaving a bowl of soup half finished. Instead of feeding him, I had sent him away hungry.

He was growing thinner. I worried that he was running out of money and took to bringing fruit and the granola bars Jay used to like to the library. At first I left them near his table, as you might to attract shy birds. When I saw he was eating the food, I moved it closer to my desk. When he stopped by to scoop up an apple in his long, thin, freckled fingers, I said, "Isn't it getting a little cold in your tent?" I tried not to sound worried. Somewhere out there he had escaped a mother.

He looked at me as though a statue had come to life—Don Carlos or the Friendly Giant. Eric fled to his table and would not approach the feeding tray until I returned it to his side of the room.

I was wrong about his escaping from his mother. It was his mother who had left him. I told you the novel was the story of my life. Eric described a garden party given by the parents. There were candles in little paper bags, outlining beds of roses and delphinium. A bar was set up in front of a dark green yew hedge. The bartender knew everyone and what they liked to drink. Wade and I had employed such a bartender. He appeared at all our friends' parties, dispensing drinks like an indulgent parent. There was a couple in the novel who was especially close to the boy's parents. The boy's mother was having an affair with the man. Eric had made both the mother and her lover hateful. I read this chapter while Eric was washing his clothes in the restroom. He had taken to leaving his laundry draped over the fixtures just before the library closed. In the morning he was there early to gather it up. The basin must have been too small for his jeans, for I often found the toilet bowl full of soapy water tinted an inky blue. I resented the way Eric assumed the affair was the mother's fault. He had made the mother and her lover villains when they might have been more interesting as victims.

Larry and I watched his wife, Maria, and my husband, Wade, begin their affair. Although they were unusually tender and considerate to-

ward us, we were children left out of a game. My first luncheon with
Larry was to talk over what was going on between Wade and Maria.
Larry wanted to divorce Maria. I felt he was being hasty. I wasn't sure
how much of his impatience was anger over Maria's unfaithfulness and
how much was boredom, with its yearning for a crisis however painful.
Even then Larry was talking about getting away and starting over.

During the luncheons that followed—and they were nothing more
than luncheons—we entertained ourselves by pretending we could go
anywhere we wished, that Scott Fitzgerald was wrong when he said
there were no second acts in American lives. Larry told me he dreamed
of going to Alaska. He was drawn by the idea of adventure. To me,
Alaska seemed a blank page.

Wade and Maria stopped seeing one another, but we had made their
rules our rules. Many secret clubs have been started because people
have found themselves excluded from someone else's secret club. After
the divorce, we came to Alaska and we both found what we expected.

In December we had one storm after another. By now I was not alone
in my concern over Eric. When the weather was bad, the sheriff made
a point of driving by and checking the boy's tent. People speculated on
how much longer he would hold out. It was late morning now before he
warmed up enough to remove his jacket. He often skipped his bath, so
there were fewer opportunities for me to read his novel. Still, I saw
enough to know the parents were divorced and the mother had left with
her lover for La Jolla. I thought of her there in a house on one of the
hills outside the city. She would have a view of the Pacific and a garden
in which, even at this final time of year, flowers bloom. But the view
and the flowers are nothing to her, something invented too soon or too
late to be useful. Her son is in Alaska. The letters she writes to him are
unopened. Reading Eric's novel was like looking down a long hallway
of mirrors.

Each day Eric looked paler and thinner, as though he were erasing
himself along with the words he wrote and rewrote. His eyes were
watery and he had a hacking cough that disturbed the readers in the
library. He was writing less, and some mornings he would cross his
arms and put his head down. Was there ever a time in your life when
you were more protected than when you and your classmates had your
heads down on your crossed arms and were watched over by a teacher?

When I saw he was no longer restocking his woodpile, I was afraid he would be leaving soon. Driving by the park one morning, I would find the tent gone. I decided to ask him to have dinner with me so that I could plead my case; if he forgave me, it would be almost like Jay forgiving me.

I was right about his taking off. He was leaving the next morning, he said, and agreed to the dinner. I suppose he thought now that he was going away, it was safe to be with me.

We left the library together. Eric folded himself awkwardly into my small Japanese car. "What kind of mileage do you get?" he asked.

"Thirty-five, somewhere around there." We talked about the car and the weather until we were settled in a high-backed booth at the restaurant, where we had a little too much privacy. I ordered wine, a crabmeat frittata, and a spinach salad. Eric asked for beer and a hamburger. He was trying not to be an expensive guest; he wanted to owe me as little as possible.

We had been in one another's company for weeks. I had read his novel and cleaned up his bath water, but shut into the booth with him I was self-conscious. In awkward situations I am appalled to find myself saying things that are too personal. It is why we talk so much, knowing what confidences silence brings out. "I read your novel," I confessed. "It was so much like my own life. I have a son your age working on the oil rigs in Texas. I suppose it's like your coming here to Alaska."

"I knew you had been reading my stuff, but I didn't care that much. You've been really nice to me. I came to Alaska because I wanted to get as far away as I could. Everyone was talking about my mother. People felt sorry for me. Everyone in the family—her side, too—was having Dad and me over for dinner and sympathy. They sat around all evening trying to figure out why my mother would do something like that.

"That's why I started the novel; I thought if I wrote about it, I could understand it, only it's all coming out of *my* head and not hers, so I'm not getting anywhere. I don't think I've gone back far enough. She used to talk a lot about when she was a girl. It was really kind of interesting stuff. Her grandfather came over here from Ireland; he was related to Parnell. I've even thought about going over there. I mean, they're still fighting in Northern Ireland. I wonder what she'd think about my doing that? At the university here I met someone who knows someone in New York with connections to the IRA. First, I've got to get some money together."

Much too eagerly I said, "You could stay here in Anchorage. My husband, Larry, could help you find a job." If his mother could not have him, perhaps I could, but even as I made the offer I felt I was asking for something belonging to someone else.

"No," he said, "I'm going to New Mexico. I've got a friend there who can get me a job with him on a ranch."

Evidently there was no possibility of my being a friend.

"I thought I could be on my own here, but you can't get away from people."

Did Eric mean me? Not only my son but the sons of other women wanted to elude me. "Ireland," I said angrily. "You're being a romantic. You don't know anything about what's happening there; it isn't the same IRA and anyhow, it's none of your business. You could be killed."

He shrugged. It wasn't bravado; he didn't care. Somewhere on the top of an oil rig in Texas was Jay shrugging at the chance he was taking? "Why don't you care?" I asked, full of sudden impatience.

His smile suggested there was no point in trying to explain to me. He would shut me up like his mother's unopened letters. I wouldn't be shut up. "You have no right to punish her." I must have been talking too loudly because he looked around to see if anyone were listening. "Who are you to judge," I said. "You don't know the facts. People are entitled to their happiness."

"Listen," he said nervously, "thanks for the dinner. I have to go now and get my things together. I'm getting an early flight out."

He refused my offer of a ride back to the park. He wanted to say goodbye to a friend in the bookstore down the street. I watched him leave the restaurant. I saw that Jay and Eric formed a consensus. I paid the bill and walked out of the restaurant by myself. In the sky, bands of color were expanding and contracting in heavy breaths. I hurried to my car to get out of the cold, but once inside I stayed parked, watching the northern lights form a frigid rainbow. What kind of peace could come from a sign like that?

On my way to the library the next morning, I tried not to look at the empty space in the park where Eric's tent had been. Mrs. Murchis came in, very excited with an acknowledgment from Mrs. Brezhnev, in

Russian, on paper a strange shade of gray. We studied the perplexing alphabet. It seemed right that the message should be mysterious. After she left, I addressed an envelope to Eric's mother. I remembered her address from the unopened letters. I wrote that her son had been working each day at my library, that he was fine and leaving the cold Alaskan winter to be with a friend in New Mexico. I said I knew how forgetful sons that age could be about writing. He had mentioned her to me and so I had taken the liberty of sending a few lines.

First Light

There has been, lately, a shifting of books. Sheldon Ferrell—professor emeritus of economics, fly fisherman, and enemy of banks—has moved from his home near the university to the northern part of the state, where he has a fishing shack on the Sandy River. He wife has been dead for four years. Had it not been for his need to browse through every one of his several thousand books before he packed them, looking for God knows what, he might have moved sooner. There was another reason for his delay. His daughter, Gail, is going through a difficult time.

Gail is driving up to spend the summer with her father. She and her husband, Stuart, have been divorced. In the back of her car is a box of children's picture books, which over the years she has written and illustrated. For reassurance, she keeps her accomplishments near at hand. Gail's books are sprightly tales of precocious raccoons and saucy squirrels. In her purse is a letter from her horrified editor turning down a story for five-year-olds in which a fox, caught in a trap, bites off its leg. Gail doesn't know what has come over her.

Gail's divorced husband, Stuart, has mingled his law books with his girlfriend's vegetarian cookbooks and has headed west. The girlfriend is widely compassionate. She is sorry for little calves and lambs and will not eat them. She is only a little less sorry for the wife and sons Stuart is leaving behind.

Gail and Stuart's twin sons, Pete and Chris, helped to clear out the family home. They moved several cartons of their childhood books to their apartments. They regret having to shift the books. It was pleasant to think of their childhood intact on the shelves of their parents' home. Chris has given up his job with an ad agency and Pete has left law school. Together they have opened a tennis and ski shop. They meet each morning for breakfast and often call across the store to one another, relieved to find the other still there.

We can guess how things are going to go for Stuart. (Frankly, I'm not sorry; he said some unforgivable things to Gail.) The boys will find they have a flair for business and do well. It is Gail who needs our attention. She is embarrassed to be running home to her eighty-year-old parent, who likes his solitude and is busily engaged in finishing the book on which he has been working for forty years. The book, *Behind Locked Doors: A History of Banking,* has been a comfort to him. It is a relief for a scrupulous man to settle early in life on the particular sin he will spend his days attacking.

Now that her husband has relinquished the job, Gail is counting on her father to take care of her. Things are out of control. Last week a bird flew down her chimney and into her living room, where it hurled itself against the white walls, marking them with a sooty script that appeared to spell out a warning. The bird was charged with so urgent a need to escape, it terrified Gail, who is used to the docile animals she puts in her books. She was about to call the police when the bird fell lifeless to the floor, claws frozen into hooks. Gail hopes the woods around her father's cabin will supply, for her stories, animals that are more genial.

Her father called several times to check on the condition of her car and the route she would take, forgetting how familiar to her the road is. As a child she had traveled it with her parents. When the boys were growing up, she and Stuart took them to the fishing shack for camping vacations. The trip is just as she remembers. The cities, first large, then small, disappear. She drives through villages with feed and hardware stores and red brick town halls and post offices built in the thirties of yellow brick in which, should one look inside, there are murals of outsized men heroically going about some mundane work. At last there is nothing but woods of unconvincing scrub oak and jack pine, haphazard trees that might have been constructed by a child from twigs and bits of green sponge. When she comes to the mile of trail leading to her father's cabin, she turns into it like a fearful animal into its burrow.

Gail need not be afraid of unsettling her father's routine. Sheldon welcomes having his daughter where he can keep an eye on her. He believes she will be no trouble, having always been a quiet, compliant girl who could amuse herself. Sheldon is finding the nights lonelier than he anticipated. The whippoorwill that appeared on his rooftop each evening at twilight has deserted him. He has made up Gail's bed and placed a bouquet of wild iris and field daisies on her dresser.

Sheldon's only fear is that his daughter will keep him from working by bringing with her a miasma of misery which will settle about the corners of the cabin like the ground fogs that rise from the river on chilly nights. When he sees Gail walking toward the cabin dragging her light luggage, his fear is confirmed.

Gail drops the luggage on the floor of the cabin and embraces her father, who feels to her less substantial than she remembers or needs. "Well, aren't you snug here," she says in what she thinks passes for a cheerful voice. The cabin is much as she remembers it except for the addition of her father's books, which are stacked in uneven pillars against the walls so that within the structure of the cabin there is a second dwelling, made of books, in which they will live. There is a stone fireplace and dark oak furniture with cushions that smell of damp and have not been reupholstered since Gail's childhood. A faint imprint suggests a pattern of red flowers on the tan background, but that might be just a memory. Without looking, she reaches for the tin ashtray that is always on the mantel. Trying to ignore her father's disapproval of her smoking, she sinks into one of the chairs, feeling the familiar lumpiness of its cushion, and lights a cigarette, which she badly needs. Instinctively, she kicks off her shoes and tucks her legs under her, the way she sat as a child. "It must be awful to have an aging daughter turn up on your doorstep?"

"I was looking forward to your coming," Sheldon says graciously, "but I worried about your driving up alone. Did you bring something warm to wear?" A frost that morning had turned the new June grass white and stiff. "You're looking a little on the thin side. We'll grill a sirloin tonight." He is trying to be both mother and father.

Gail thinks how lucky her sons are to be twins. People seldom concentrate on just one of them. "How is your book coming?" she asks, hoping to divert attention from herself.

"Not badly. If I have a couple of years left in me, I'll be able to complete the book. The university press has expressed an interest." Sheldon hurries over this. Later in the evening, when there will be a nice, long stretch of time, he has planned to give Gail a detailed description of the chapter on which he is working. "How about you? Have you started work on something?"

"Lately I seem to be writing kiddie Gothics."

He listens gravely. "It's never too soon to teach children. You might write a little story about the Federal Reserve."

Gail appreciates her father's interest in her friendless skunks and hyperactive mice, but his suggestion puzzles her.

"Start with squirrels lending out nuts." He notices the expression on Gail's face and changes the subject. "How are the boys?"

"They're fine. The store's a great success."

"I don't like the idea of their taking a bank loan." His principles keep Sheldon from having anything to do with banks. His wife was forbidden a checking account, and Gail can remember her mother's embarrassment at having to carry envelopes of cash around to pay the monthly bills.

"You mentioned a steak," she says.

After dinner she follows her father outside. All during the meal she has been aware of the sound of the river as it washes against logs and nudges the small, reluctant stones along the riverbed. Now she can smell the rich, pungent odor of water that has known hidden places. Years ago her father built a platform cantilevered over the river where he could stand and cast for trout. She sits cross-legged on the platform, the rough wood catching at the backs of her city nylons, and watches her father send his fishing line thirty feet upstream with a smart snap of his wrist.

A mink swims against the current, gliding unafraid toward them, its slick head parting the water, its beady eyes trying to decide what they are but not really caring. Her father turns to her with a complicit smile and they watch together as the mink loops back and forth until it loses interest in them and, slipping beneath the water, disappears. She thinks she might write a story about a family of mink. She will draw them as sophisticated and rather snobbish in their mink coats. She sees them going out for dinner to an elegant restaurant where they are served live baby ducks in a rich sauce. Gail is not at all pleased to have such a detail appear in her head.

She turns to her father, "Is the stone castle still there?" It is not a castle but an enormous stone lodge built on the river years ago by an auto magnate as a hunting and fishing retreat. When he fenced his six hundred acres, local people, who had hunted and fished on the property as long as they could remember, were furious. On the evening of the day the lodge was completed it was burned to the ground. The interior was gutted but the walls stood. The man never returned.

When Gail was a child, she and her father often canoed the four-mile stretch of river to the lodge. After she had been allowed to explore the ruins, her father would work the canoe back upstream against the strong current. The stone lodge had remained in the back of her mind as something she had owned, as she had never owned anything since.

"Haven't seen the stone lodge in years," Sheldon tells her. "Couldn't manage to get a canoe ten feet back upstream these days, much less four miles." Then, as if he could read her mind, "And don't you try it. You haven't been in a canoe in years."

The warning is familiar. As a child, she was forever being reminded by her father to be careful. She was allowed no bicycle; horseback riding was forbidden; she had not even learned to swim because her father thought the current was treacherous. Her father's fear troubled her; it was not just overprotectiveness for an only child, but some lack of trust in providence, or worse, a belief in a malevolence—not so much that he was protecting her as that he couldn't protect her.

The sun has fallen and darkness takes over the spaces between the pine trees. A penetrating layer of cold air creeps toward them from the river. In the distance there is the convulsed cry of a loon. Inside the cabin her father makes a fire; a primitive answer to their primitive fears. He sends Gail to her room for dry shoes and to the kitchen to make tea and then beats her at three straight games of chess while explaining how the Federal Reserve goes about rediscounting.

Getting ready for bed, Gail finds, for the first time since Stuart told her he wanted a divorce, she is looking forward to the morning. While her father is occupied with his book, she will take the canoe downstream a half mile or so and see if she can paddle it back against the current. If she works at it each day, by the end of the summer she will be able to make her way to the stone lodge. She has what she hasn't had in months—a plan.

Something glides across her room, a shape blacker than the darkness. It passes over her head and disappears through the wide crack beneath her door. She quickly stuffs the crack with a towel to keep the bat from returning to her room. They can search for it tomorrow. She considers a story in which a family of bats takes over a house each night when the family retires. The bats read the family's books and perch on their furniture. She will draw them as benign, amiable, petal-eared, bright-eyed creatures, so children will grow up unafraid of bats, but as she drifts off to sleep, one of the storybook bats flies into a child's room and tangles itself in the child's hair.

After breakfast Gail makes some excuse to her father about going out to sketch, receiving his cautionary advice to wear a hat against the June sun. After his reluctant release, she walks down to the river and drags the canoe from under the platform. It is covered with spiderwebs that stick to her fingers. She begins to invent a story about a spider who goes for a ride in a boat. She dresses him in a blue-and-white-striped bathing suit with many pantlegs. Before she can stop it, the spider, who cannot swim, tumbles into the water.

Gail climbs carefully into the canoe, steadying herself by laying the paddle horizontally across the gunwales as her father had taught her to do years before. The pull of the current is stronger than she remembers. She works at avoiding logs and sandbars. After a half mile, she digs her paddle into the riverbed and shifts the canoe around to face upstream. She begins paddling as hard as she can. After a short distance, she sees that for every foot she has gained against the current, she has lost two. Her arms have no strength in them. In desperation she eases herself out of the canoe and, hanging onto it, begins to drag it back against the current, thankful for the stretch of shallow water.

As she wades the river, she feels the chill of little springs around her ankles. The tug of the current on the sand is like a rug being pulled gently from beneath her feet. Her jeans cling wetly to her legs. She thinks of Thoreau, how he had stripped to shirt and hat and walked, as she is walking, along the middle of a stream. She has always wondered how he managed so successfully to give himself the impression he lived alone in the wilderness when his friends and family were only a mile or two away. Tag alder and willow bend protectively over her. A sociable dragonfly alights on her shoulder. Red-winged blackbirds call from a patch of leatherleaf. The river looks as if it ends in a stockade of pine trees, and then she rounds a bend and finds another stretch opening out ahead of her. By the time she reaches the cabin, her legs are numb from the cold water. Planning the next day's trip, she climbs out and walks back barefoot over the rough grass to the cabin.

Her father takes fright at the sight of her soaked jeans. "I was sketching dragonflies," she tells him.

The days organize themselves into an easy routine. Each morning she puts on a bathing suit under her jeans and shirt and sets out for the lodge, leaving her father to wreak vengeance upon bankers who, oblivious of the impending danger, sip their coffee and shuffle through piles of crisp paper. By the end of the first week, Gail is able to paddle a full mile against the current.

The second week takes her through a cedar swamp. It is late June now, but cool breezes blunder out of the swamp as if winter snows might still lie hidden among the exposed roots of the trees. The shadows of the cedars and tamaracks lie in dark bars across the river. Sometimes the canoe scares up a heron. The great gray-blue bird stands among the cedars silent as a stump, not even blinking his yellow eyes until she is almost upon him, then he shakes out his wings like a cloak and rises into the air, neck folded, legs trailing. By the end of the week he has grown accustomed to her. If she approaches quietly, she is able to watch him as he lifts a foot, holds it up for a count of ten, puts it down, and lifts the other. He is foraging for crayfish. Perhaps a story about a heron, she thinks. She tries sketching him when she gets back to the cabin, but the bird has so much elegant stealth she can not turn him into anything useable.

The muscles in Gail's arms stop aching. Her father remarks on how tan and healthy-looking she is growing. "You're a different person." He is delighted and believes it is his doing. Their lives blend. After lunch they read or nap, her father stretched out in his room and she in hers, with no sound but the river. In the afternoons she goes into the nearby town to get the papers and the mail. They know her now and she has only to smile and she is handed what is hers. The boys send cheerful letters, their relief in her adjustment evident. Business is good, they write. Casually, they mention a note from Stuart, who complains of back trouble and the high price of California real estate. Comparing her life with his, Gail finds she is sorry for Stuart. The boys promise to come up the end of August for a week of fishing. She plans on surprising them by taking them down to the lodge in the canoe.

After an early dinner, she sits by the river in the long, light twilight while her father stands on the platform and casts for trout. Nighthawks are in free fall, startling Gail with their recklessness. Her father fishes with dry flies, using a hook without a barb, throwing back the trout he catches. Each time a trout is released, Gail holds her breath while it rights itself, waits for a moment assessing its luck, and then with a flick of its tail, escapes. One night there is a thunderstorm and the electricity fails. It is too warm for a fire and mice have nibbled away the candles, so Gail and her father sit in the darkness, visible to one another only when lightning strikes. The sound of the rain on the roof of the cabin drowns out speech. They have never been closer.

The last week of July, when she has worked the canoe to within a mile of the stone lodge, her father discovers what she is doing. A hatch has broken out on the river and, hearing the trout jump for the small insects, he is lured away from his book. He reaches the platform with his trout rod just as Gail pulls up in the canoe. He stares at her, red-faced, his rod upright at his side. "What are you doing in that canoe?"

"I thought I'd like to see the stone castle again." Intimidated, she reverts to the childish name for the lodge.

"Impossible. You know how far that is. You'd have a four-mile return upstream. You wouldn't make that in a hundred years; you were never good at paddling a canoe."

"I've been paddling every day. I got within a mile of the lodge today. Another week and I know I'll be able to manage the whole distance."

"There are holes in the last mile of the stream that are over your head. Suppose the canoe tips. You'd drown."

"Why didn't you teach me to swim?" She has not meant to accuse him.

"Gail, it's very pleasant having you here. This can be a lonely place and I enjoy your company, but I must be free to finish my book. I haven't much time left. I certainly can't concentrate if I have to worry about where you are every minute of the day and whether or not you are in some sort of danger."

"Dad," she is pleading, "I'm a grown woman."

"You are still my daughter and I am responsible for you. I want you to promise me you won't take the canoe out again."

His love is as intimidating as ever; she agrees. Walking alone back to the cabin, she sees by her promise she has assented to the malevolence in which her father believes.

At dinner, Sheldon, the gracious victor, tells her, "Tomorrow I'll give myself a vacation from the book and we can drive over to the inn. We'll have a decent meal and you can look through the shops."

This was what she and her mother used to do as a treat when she was a child. Why should her rewards and punishments be meted out by others? Her father sees she is reconsidering her promise. After dinner he mentions a pain in his chest and decides to skip the evening's fishing. There is no chess either. Instead, Sheldon sits with a book in front of him, ostentatiously not turning the pages. Gail suffers even more than he means her to.

Later, alone in her room, she stands at the window. There is a full moon and Gail sees much more than she thought she could. She looks at the river which now belongs to her father; as though it were a dangerous toy, he has taken it away from her. Her father will watch her closely; there will be no more opportunities to take out the canoe. She could defy him, but when she rehearses the scene—angry words, the slamming of the cabin door, the march down to the river—she thinks it would be more than she could manage.

She hears her father snoring faintly in the bedroom next to hers like a watchman asleep on the other side of a prison door. Gail opens the window and, heady with surreptitious freedom, climbs out, stifling a giggle at the absurdity of her exit. She heads for the river and the canoe. In the moonlight the surface of the river has fractured into shards of broken light; the very act of riding upon it is astonishing.

At this midnight hour, Gail, nervous at being the only creature on earth, is relieved to see the mink cut across her path. Like herself, the mink is intent on some secret business. When she reaches the swamp, she finds a ground fog spread delicately over the water like a lace tablecloth. She slows the canoe, trying to recall where the stumps and deadheads are; it is a kind of blindman's bluff. She puts her hand into the fog and feels its bodiless chill. The canoe carries her out of the fog and between high, sandy banks that still hold something back from the river. She knows the lodge is close. She can tell from the swiftness of the current that she is gliding over the deep holes about which her father warned her, and she tightens her grip on the paddle. She knows that when she returns, working her way upstream, should she lose control of the canoe in the strong current, she won't be able to brace the paddle against the river bottom. The darkness on either side of her falls away; the bluffs are gone and there in the clearing is the lodge, its cracked walls substantial, even impressive, in the weak light of the moon.

Gail pulls the canoe onto a spit of sand. As she approaches the lodge, she can see the empty rooms are carpeted with grass. She remembers a trip to Italy and a walk she and Stuart took in the Forum. She remembers the green grass against the pink and gray of the ancient stones and thinks the world is full of alluring ruins, so lovely you forget their warning.

Frosted Queen Anne's lace and silver thistles cover the clearing and have entered the lodge like pushy visitors. There is nothing depressing here; the violence and the scars are concealed by all that has happened since. She moves from room to room. It is just as she remembers it. She tries to recall the childish game she played there while her father fished on the bank: it was a kind of housekeeping—setting stone tables with leaves and twigs, ordering about imaginary children. Gail feels at home in this shell that was once a house. She thinks she might write a story about the animals who live here: meadow voles, squirrels, perhaps a fox or woodchuck. She waits for some intimidating, shocking detail to intrude on her story; none does. She remembers the blue heron starting up, sliding over her like a great gray-blue shadow, its wings beating against the air, until it had lifted itself above the trees and beyond. She is embarrassed to think how for her own purposes she has reduced the animals in her books to something so much less than they are.

She selects a pebble, a talisman, from the crumbling walls and puts it in her pocket. She sees the lodge is the best kind of shelter, a shelter of open doors and windows.

Gail works the canoe back against the current with the open-mouthed holes lying in ambush beneath her. Should the canoe tip, the holes will swallow her up as her father has warned. An old feeling of helplessness makes her break her stroke. The canoe slips sideways and she is drifting downstream. She gouges the water with her paddle, boring through its dissolving surface, and pushes against nothing that holds. The canoe spins slowly around and around, playful while she is desperate. Downstream the dark shadow of a pine extends out from the shore. She is able to glide the wayward canoe toward the tree and reach with her paddle for its rooted stability. The canoe holds. She turns the canoe around, pushes off, and inches upstream, digging into the water with firm strokes. After she passes the high banks, she is back in shallow water. She lifts the paddle from one side of the canoe to the other, meeting the current and moving the canoe along.

Everything is familiar until she sees ahead of her in the stream a dark shape; nothing ghostly, the creature is solid, and should you rest your hand against its flank, warm. Gail slows the canoe to keep from startling the deer, which has swung its head around and is looking in her direction. Gail knows deer once went about only in the daylight. Since man has decreased their world, the deer live the freer part of their lives at night. Gail imagines them wandering nimble-footed and cautious through whatever is left over for them from the day. The deer moves across the stream, disappearing into the woods to become a shadow among other shadows.

Gail beaches the canoe at the landing and walks toward the cabin. In the morning she will tell her father what she has done. Unlike the deer, she is not content to live in the half-light of stars and moons and planets. In the east she sees the silhouettes of the pines soften and brighten and their dark shapes fall away into light.

The Dogs in Renoir's Garden

"There's an extra charge each month if you don't use their furniture."
May Elger put down the tortoiseshell shoehorn and looked around her
small room. She thought of the little collection of furniture as choices
she might have made from a burning house; not the most valuable
things, but the first to come to mind. They had allowed her to have her
little satinwood writing table with the ormolu mounts and a graceful,
gilded cane chair. The chest that held her clothes—the few she
needed—was Empire. On the chest was a Lowestoft armorial plate,
which her doctor insisted on using for an ashtray. Snuffing out his
cigarettes, he was eroding the honey gold on the crest, but she never
corrected him. He was the one who pronounced her sentences.

Only the bed belonged to the nursing home. They insisted on it
remaining. Who could blame them for believing she would need it as
she grew older? The evidence was all around them. With its bulky,
mechanical contrivances that could manipulate your body into infinite
angles, the bed, set down in the midst of the delicate furniture, looked
like a small factory.

Her little Renoir painting which she missed most was not allowed
her. The insurance company had pronounced the security at the nursing
home inadequate. May considered that ironic. She had found the security so effective that in the year and ten months of her stay, and in spite
of the unlocked doors, she had never ventured out of the home by
herself. But then, her daughter had placed her there, and May was
always ready to accept the appraisal of others.

"Why wouldn't it be *less* when you use your own furniture?" May's friend, Ethel, grasped the slight conversational thread and held on. She saw that May had lost weight. The red-and-white silk dress hung on her waning frame like a large flag draped over a small casket. May's daughter, Susan, obviously hadn't bothered to buy anything new for her mother. But then, she never bought clothes for herself, or if she did, they all looked the same. Susan was a large, bony creature who carried a purse like a suitcase and had a habit of sitting with her legs apart and her feet planted firmly on the ground. She took after her father, who had died of a heart attack in one of the worst November storms on record after refusing to leave a duck blind until he had bagged his limit.

"They charge you because they have to store their own furniture." May was standing in front of the mirror, loosening her pearl earrings. She wasn't used to wearing them and had forgotten the aggressive way they nipped her ear lobes. Averting her eyes from the ghost in the mirror with the pale, blanched look of a weed working its way up through layers of mulch, she tried to recall her last outing from the nursing home. What a hateful word "outing" was, she thought, conjuring up images of helpless babies in prams and little old ladies being aired like musty sheets.

It must have been four or five months since Susan and Richard had taken her out for Easter dinner. An evening of disasters, all of them of her own making, as Susan had been quick to point out to her mother. May was surprised Susan had given Ethel permission for this luncheon.

"The Merles finally had that old privet hedge yanked out," Ethel told May. It was pleasant to pretend they still had their suburban street in common. The two women had been next-door neighbors for thirty years. Ethel was relieved May never asked about her own home. Susan and Richard had moved in, announcing to Ethel over the brick wall that separated the two gardens, "We're here to keep an eye on things until Mother comes back."

If they expected May to come back, Ethel wondered, why were so many of May's things being carried out the front door? Ethel had seen a well-known auctioneer leave with two large cartons, and one Saturday morning a half-dozen antique dealers in full cry filled up their vans and drove triumphantly away. The most troubling of all had been picking up the *New York Times* and finding in an auction notice on the art page a picture of the little Renoir painting of a garden that had hung in May's living room. Over the years May had lovingly planted in her own garden all the flowers that appeared in the painting. Walking outdoors, you walked right into the Renoir. It seemed a sacrilege that someone else should own it.

Then there were the dogs. Susan raised German shepherds. You could see them through the windows, careening around the rooms, skidding on May's parquet floors, May's priceless Oriental rugs dangling from their muzzles. When Ethel was in her yard, the dogs peered over the wall smiling their clown's smile at her, their tongues lolling out between long, pointed white teeth. The stench from their feces, which no one bothered to bury from one week to the next, was so strong it was impossible to open your windows.

The dogs had ravaged May's garden, uprooting the lilies and irises. They jousted at one another with long stalks of May's delphinium held between their teeth. They snapped off peony and poppy blossoms and gobbled them down whole.

Ethel hadn't signed the petition that had gone up and down the street asking for the dogs' removal. For May's sake she tried to remain friends with Susan. But Ethel knew Susan would certainly be angry with her if she knew she was taking her mother out to lunch. Ethel had implied to May that Susan knew all about the luncheon, but of course she didn't.

Ethel had broached the subject to Susan, trying not to show her impatience at having to ask permission from someone half her age. "It's been such a lovely summer, what would you think of my running your mother over to the club for a little lunch?"

Susan had immediately quashed the idea. "Isn't that thoughtful of you. But you'd never be able to manage Mother. Richard and I, between the two of us, could hardly handle her last Easter."

That had not been reassuring. Ethel had often looked out of her bedroom window into May's yard while Susan yanked the big black-and-tan dogs about in their choke collars, nearly throttling them. What was it about her frail ninety-five-pound mother that made her so unmanageable? When Ethel visited May in the nursing home each Thursday afternoon, she seemed perfectly clear-headed and sensible. Ethel

knew May had problems with drinking. But surely that could be han-
dled? It was unconscionable that Susan should allow those great beasts
of dogs in the house, but not her own mother.

Ethel looked at May standing doubtfully in front of the mirror and
felt a surge of affection. What confidences had gone back and forth
over the brick wall. The grieving over the bits and pieces the doctors
had pruned from their aging bodies; Ethel's mastectomy and later,
May's hysterectomy. Susan's marriage to Richard, who had been the
dog warden in their suburb. Ethel's son leaving his wife and four children to marry his tennis pro. And the deaths.

"You look very posh," Ethel said, envying May's trim figure beneath
the too-large dress. "Yesterday a snotty saleslady at Saks tried to tell
me I needed a size sixteen." Ethel looked at her watch. The nursing
home made her claustrophobic. "I suppose we'd better go. Size sixteen
or not, I've been thinking about an avocado-and-crabmeat salad all
morning. After one o'clock the ripe avocados are all gone and you get
those stringy ones that are hard as a rock."

On the way to the club, May sat looking greedily out of the car
window. It was like watching an old movie. Just as you reconciled
yourself to having forgotten it, something familiar would flash on the
screen and you would set to work all over again trying to remember
how the story went. They were only a few blocks from her home, but
May saw that Ethel was not going out of her way to pass it. Probably a
kindness on her part, a desire not to rub salt in the wound. May con-
tented herself with looking at the other peoples' homes. Even that was
painful, suggesting as they did the exotic process of a daily life.

When they reached the country club, Eddie, the doorman, seemed
genuinely glad to see May. "Mrs. Elger, you picked yourself a beautiful day. They're serving on the terrace. You'd enjoy that." May was
grateful for his discretion in not mentioning how long it had been since
he had last seen her there. He helped her out of the car and guided her
attentively through the door. Servants had always tended to baby her
and she had encouraged the little game of appearing to be dependent on
those who were dependent on her.

Ethel would have preferred an obscure table in the grill to eating on
the terrace where they would be on display—not that she expected to
run into Susan. Susan despised the country club. She had not set foot

there since her high-school years when she captained the swim team; only kennel clubs for her.

But once seated at one of the pink wrought-iron tables, Ethel put her misgivings aside. Perhaps it was atavistic, but she believed strongly that nothing unpleasant could happen when you were under the beneficence of the sun. And then, eating outdoors, no matter how formal the service, remained a childhood treat.

May looked past the red geraniums and neatly clipped boxwood to the large blue saucer of the swimming pool and the smaller blue circle of the children's wading pool. In the days when their youngsters were growing up, nursemaids in crisp white uniforms watched over them. Now, the mothers seemed to keep track of their own toddlers. She thought of how often she had left Susan in a nursemaid's care. Now, Susan was reciprocating. But it was foolish to feel guilty about nursemaids—British nannies had produced Winston Churchill and Sir Kenneth Clark.

May turned her glance to the golf course with its alternating stretches of open lawn and thickets of trees. In the distance she could make out green clouds of willows lowering over a tiny creek. She and Ethel had sat on the terrace in the summer twilight sipping long, cool drinks and waiting for their husbands to finish their golf game. She remembered the sharp cries of the nighthawks as they plummeted from the sky, recovering themselves at the very moment you lost hope.

Ethel glanced at the tables around them, relieved to find no one she knew, no one to come over and ask clumsily of May, "Where have you been keeping yourself?" It was a young crowd. "The girls all look naked," she said to May. Their shirts were sleeveless and unbuttoned halfway down their chests. They were braless and their nipples showed through the flimsy summer fabric.

"I remember a strapless evening gown you wore to the Beaux Arts Ball that left very little to the imagination." May was actually laughing.

Ethel began to think the afternoon would be possible after all, when a waitress, neat in a uniform with a pink apron, stood at the table, smiling pleasantly. "May I bring you something to drink?"

It was a moment Ethel had rehearsed. She couldn't refuse May a drink; that would be too obvious. What she had decided to do was order a wine spritzer for herself. It was rude to order before her guest, but she hoped May would take the hint and have something light. But before Ethel could order, May was smiling innocently up at the waitress and saying brightly, "I'll have a double martini, straight up."

May had decided there would probably be a chance for no more than one drink. It might be her only drink for several more months. Even if Ethel gave her the opportunity, she resolved not to order a second one. If all went well today, Ethel might take her to luncheon another time. There might be many afternoons like this one. Ethel might tell Susan how well her mother had behaved. Or she might say something to someone in the trust department of the bank or to her lawyer, who no longer answered her letters even though he had been a lifelong friend and had gone trout fishing with her husband every spring.

"They've turned one of the private dining rooms into a backgammon room," Ethel told her.

"Which one?" She was concentrating on the waitress coming slowly across the terrace with two glasses balanced on a silver tray—a tall goblet and a shorter one. The drinks were certainly theirs. She turned her attention to what Ethel was saying.

"The room that had the blue toile wallpaper with the cross-eyed cupids all over it. Conway Studios did it. Remember? And the fake Limoges ashtrays with the gold bees that looked like seagulls."

The waitress put the frosty glasses down on pink paper coasters with the club emblem imprinted in green. May curled her fingers around the stem of her glass like a baby grasping its mother's finger.

Ethel studied her menu. When she looked up, May had emptied her drink. "What are you going to have?" she asked hastily. "They have those stuffed mushrooms you always liked."

May was appalled at her empty glass. For a moment she thought someone else had emptied it. But no, she felt the door opening. With it came the feeling things were possible, all kinds of things, one day different from another. Other rooms. Other streets. Other cities and countries.

She had begun drinking too much after her husband's death. Unable to eat dinner alone in the large, empty house where forty years of conversations lay about, unextinguished, like hundreds of small ruinous fires, she took to eating out. Alone, night after night in restaurants and clubs, she felt peripheral. It required so much effort to keep your glance from intruding on that of another diner's. Then there were the salad bars. Even some of the very good restaurants had them. She hated the coarse chunks of iceberg lettuce, the fake bacon bits that tasted like minced shoe leather, the slimy, semen-like bean sprouts, and the messy ladles you dredged up from the dressing pits. She hated the way they pretended to give you choices.

After three or four drinks, waiters and waitresses had seemed kindly. Other diners returned her friendly nods. The food, when she remembered to eat it, was appetizing. Possibilities suggested themselves to her: friends she might call, an exhibition at the museum she wanted to see.

But when those dinners were over, there was the difficulty of getting herself home. When her driver's license had been suspended, Susan had insisted she see her doctor. The doctor had patiently explained that as one grew older, liquor was not as easy to tolerate. She had replied that the same could be said for life, and what else did he have to offer? Then she had driven without her license and had the accident, and the parents of the boy on the bicycle sued her. Susan had consulted with the doctor and an attorney. When they had both advised the nursing home "as a temporary measure" while the suit was being settled, she had agreed.

When the waitress arrived with their food, May looked toward her glass, giving it a subtle nudge with one finger. The waitress checked Ethel's still nearly full wine goblet and returned with May's drink before Ethel could telegraph a warning look to her. Ethel began eating with little noises of pleasure as one eats in front of a small child to encourage him.

May felt Ethel's anxiety and tried to nibble at the food, but the salad Niçoise she had ordered turned out to be nothing more than tuna with a scattering of black beetle-looking olives. She saw that she must make an attempt to enter the world in which Ethel still lived and look around a little, remark on something. "Do you remember the time the house committee at the museum spent an hour arguing over how the Lukes' sculpture ought to be cleaned?" The sculpture was an enormous piece of commercial felt, a sort of giant flyswatter whose fringes trailed onto the gallery floor and tended to get stepped on.

Ethel grinned, "And they wrote to Lukes and he said he had planned on the dust and the footprints as part of the effect he wanted."

"So they couldn't touch it."

"Ethel,"—May reached her hand across the table, nearly upsetting a water glass but not noticing—"do you think we could go to the art institute some afternoon? Just to see my little Renoir? Susan said she lent it to the museum because she was afraid to have the responsibility of it at the house."

"Yes, of course," Ethel assured her, thinking of the ad in the *New York Times*.

The waitress was at the table again to clear Ethel's luncheon plate. She had another drink for May. Ethel had no idea when it was ordered. Then she saw with a sinking heart that May was pressing money into the waitress's hand. "I guess I'll have one more," May said. "The sun is making me thirsty."

Ethel fixed an icy eye on the waitress. The club had a strict rule against tipping. "May we have our check," she ordered. The check appeared with a fourth martini. Ethel hastily signed her name and rose. Too late. May had emptied her glass and seemed unable to get up from her chair. The women at the other tables looked pointedly away. Ethel tried to lift May, but for someone so slight she was surprisingly un-wieldy, like a poorly packed grocery bag.

May tried to help, using the edge of the table as a lever to raise herself, but the table began to tilt toward her, the dishes sliding and clattering. May sank helplessly down in her chair. She saw that Ethel had disappeared. Perhaps they would let her remain there. It would be pleasant in the evening when everyone had left the club, and the empty tables and chairs stood under the black sky and the moon shone on the dark water of the pool. Ever since she had entered the nursing home, May had longed to be alone at night. Although it was considered one of the best homes in the city, its construction was poor, and anonymous snores came vibrating through the walls to destroy her sleep.

Ethel returned with Eddie. "Mrs. Elger, you just lean on me now. I should never have suggested eating out here. Sun's unmercifully hot." They hoisted her awkwardly from the chair and half-dragged her across the terrace. Ethel looked straight ahead.

Eddie gently closed the car door and raised his hand in a smart salute. May was crying, the tears making pale rivulets in her foundation. Her nose needed wiping. Ethel reached for a Kleenex from the box on the dashboard and handed it to her.

May pushed it aside. "I hate Kleenex." She fumbled in her purse and brought out a linen handkerchief with a wide band of lace. "I wash out seven handkerchiefs each week in my washbasin," she said. "I iron them with my travel iron. They won't do them for me at the nursing home." The rhythm of the car soothed her. Her head began to nod.

Ethel drove cautiously, husbanding May's sleep. She would continue to see May, but she wouldn't allow herself to become involved again. Their lives were different. She, herself, still had some time left.

When they arrived at the nursing home, Ethel hurried into the lobby and pushed out one of the wheelchairs that always stood ready. It took a minute or two to awaken May and extract her from the car. An elderly gentleman resident watched but made no effort to help. Evidently he was hoarding his strength. Ethel wheeled May hastily down the corridor past the little knot of patients whose wheelchairs seemed always to be clustered around the nurse's desk, so that it was difficult to know who was watching whom. May giggled, "You're pushing me like a tea wagon."

When they reached May's room, Ethel quickly shut the door behind them and, leaving May in the wheelchair, kicked off her shoes and sank down exhausted on the bed, trying not to look up at the blank white ceiling.

"You won't tell Susan?" May asked.

"No, I won't tell her, but she may hear about it from someone at the club."

"Does she keep up my garden?"

"Yes, it looks lovely. Your delphiniums were gorgeous this June."

"I was worried. She mentioned having dogs."

"Just one. It's very well behaved."

"I'm sorry about the lunch. I don't suppose you'll want to take me out again?"

Ethel was silent, her small store of lies depleted.

"But you'll come to see me?"

"Every week. Just like I always have." When the time came, would someone come and visit *her?* Ethel swung her legs over the edge of the bed and rocked her swollen feet into her shoes.

"I do it to open the door," May risked.

Ethel gave her a strange look.

May decided after all it was best to keep these things to yourself. She realized with a sinking heart that Ethel believed in willpower.

In the late August afternoon the suburban roads were tunnels of light. Sun lay trapped under arching branches that met in the middle of the streets. Ethel felt she was swimming through gold. She was buoyant, almost euphoric, and then guilty, like someone who has ceased mourning much too soon and knows it.

As she pulled into her driveway, she looked into May's garden and saw the dogs stretched out on a bed of crushed daisies, warming themselves in the sun. Right out of Rousseau's *Peaceable Kingdom,* Ethel thought. It was a painting Ethel considered full of artful deceit. Rousseau had composed a handful of tame animals to distract you, while the wild ones waited, invisible and menacing, just behind the trees.

The Mummies of Guanajuato

It is the last day of our Mexican tour. From the balcony of our hotel room in Acapulco, I watch Elaine wavering at the edge of the ocean. She told me she once saw, in an aquarium on Cape Cod, things that have kept her out of the ocean from that day to this. Elaine wears a modest black bathing suit, appropriate for a woman of sixty, and a straw hat, purchased, with no attempt to bargain, at the Sabado Market in Mexico City. Elaine's arms and legs are fish-belly white, their flesh soft, sagging a little; but her body, firmly packed into the suit, is still shapely. When a wave washes over her bare feet, Elaine springs back as though the ocean were attacking her, as though it were one thing more she couldn't trust. She is trying to decide whether to marry Roy, who would insist on protecting her from such assaults. Although she asked my advice, I said nothing; knowing how carefully he will watch over Elaine, I don't like Roy.

The beach at Acapulco is like an overproduced opera. There is a backdrop of mountains and a blue curtain of sky. Painted onto the sky is a man in a brightly colored parachute tethered to a speedboat. An enormous white cross rises above the distant hills of Las Brisas. Like supers making an entrance, from stage right an American couple walks on, the girl wearing a bikini, the man carrying a camera. He poses the girl in the water, on the beach, stretched out on a lounge chair; each click of the camera is a consummation. A Mexican family follows. The mother and father settle in the shade. The children begin to rake their fingers through the sand as you would scratch the back of a gentle monster.

From stage left there is a procession of colorfully dressed vendors: a woman balancing on her head a tray of watermelon and mango slices, a man with an armful of gaudy dresses, another man selling puppets that caper at his side. A boy of seven or eight, belonging to one of the hawkers, runs, fully dressed, at a wave. When the wave recedes, his wet clothes cling to him like a brightly tinted skin. All that is lacking is someone to step center stage and break into an aria.

Roy and my husband, Fred, along with several members of our tour group, are in downtown Acapulco watching the young men dive off the cliffs for coins. Elaine and I stayed behind; I, to finish my travel diary, Elaine, because she thinks tourists shouldn't encourage young men to risk their lives. In her imagination she sees them plunging to their deaths: she has come to expect the worst.

I wish Elaine were a little more adventurous, a little more hopeful, although I am not one to insist we must always look on the bright side. After all, this trip to Mexico was a gift from our two sons, who wanted to do something for me when they heard (not from me, from Fred) what the eventual consequences of my illness would be. It was generous of them, but I'm not sure it was wise. Under the circumstances, every pleasure becomes a regret, and extraordinary pleasures become extraordinary regrets. When our sons were quite small, we got them a puppy, who unexpectedly developed an evil disposition. For this reason, the dog was kept away from the children. When the dog snapped at a neighbor's child, we knew we had to get rid of the dog. The night before the dog was to go, an unwitting baby-sitter allowed him into the boys' room. He jumped on and off their beds, ran around with their stuffed toys in his mouth, and at their bidding, sat up on his hind legs. The boys were delighted, but having seen what fun the dog could be, they missed him all the more.

I know Roy would not be happy to see Elaine on the beach. This morning at breakfast he warned her, "If you want to go swimming, you'd better stick to the hotel pool."

I said, "What on earth for?" Knowing I'm not on his side, Roy seldom talks to me, but I answer him all the same.

"In Mexico, the beaches are public; the hotel isn't allowed to keep outsiders away. You don't know what might be in the water."

"Salt," I suggested. Fred gave me a warning look.

I had hurt Roy's feelings. "I'm being serious," he said. He is always serious. I think there is a handful of people like Roy who keep the world from flying apart. When the kindergarten teacher gives the signal, they are the first to stretch out their little arms to make a circle. When they grow up, they write frequent letters to the editor suggesting there are ways to make things better.

From the moment our tour arrived in Mexico City, Roy took charge, finding a wheelchair for a tour member who had sprained her ankle, instructing us about the currency exchange and when we might drink the water. At one hotel he succeeded in having the assistant manager replaced—something, the bell captain confided to me, the hotel staff had been trying to effect for months. The reverse side of Roy's efficiency is an impatience with those who, unlike himself, will not take responsibility, along with the need for such people. Roy was immediately attracted to Elaine by the way she regarded her luggage as deadweight, stones too heavy to move.

There are forty of us in the tour, all from Florida retirement communities. Pleased and a little surprised still to be alive, we are ready for a good time and, with so many years of disappointments behind us, easy to please. We quickly broke down into smaller groups, depending on need or apathy. My husband, Fred, was drawn to Roy. Fred is quick to see the uselessness of trying to set things right, but he admires those who feel otherwise, and it amuses him to watch their struggles.

Roy is a widower, the only unattached man on the tour. Elaine is among four or five widows in the group. She is one of those women who tell you all about themselves the first time you meet them. Having been dragged so deeply into her life, I resigned myself to friendship; not to would have been a waste of time. Elaine has been widowed for nearly a year. Her husband, she told me, never troubled her with questions of money, so that after his death, the greediness of the world came as a shock. She was faced with income and property taxes, automobile and household insurance—expenses she had never had to pay. It was not that she couldn't afford these things, but they changed her view of the world. In the past, everything had been a series of gifts, given perhaps because of her charm or deservedness; now the whole world appeared venal.

Elaine was not a woman who easily lived alone. The radio or televi-

sion was always on. She said there was something frightening that the
background noise kept her from hearing. Although she never read
them, she renewed her husband's subscriptions to *Field and Stream* and
Sports Illustrated. "It makes me feel better," she said, "to have mail
coming for him." With the weight of the United States Post Office
behind her, it was possible at moments for Elaine to believe her husband still alive.

"It took me ten months to decide where to put my husband," Elaine
told me, leaving me with visions of his body being moved about one
room to another, like the old piece of furniture that doesn't quite fit. "I
kept him in a vault before I finally opted for earth burial; he was always
an outdoorsman. It was after I made that decision that I got up enough
courage to take this trip."

I thought, in another year or two Fred might be making a similar
trip, the widows on the tour slathering over him as over a box of
strawberries in the dead of winter.

The tour members are a congenial group, knowing that in a matter of
days we will all go our own way. Our bus driver's name is Juan; the
tour leader's name is Enrique. "Say 'good morning' to Juan," Enrique
would direct us each day as we started out.

"Good morning, Juan," we would chorus. At our age, we love playing school. Enrique explained many things. He told us the name of the
tree with the red flowers and no leaves; the brilliant blossom on the
leafless tree was encouraging. He explained that a red flag hoisted in
front of a house meant a sheep or pig had been slaughtered that day and
there was meat for sale. He told us education in his country was com-
pulsory but could not be enforced. He said Cortez was able to conquer
Mexico because the Aztecs thought he was the Plumed Serpent and you
cannot fight your own gods. As a teacher, Enrique was tolerant, with
the kind of mercy you hope for in God, excusing problems with incom-
petent hotel staff and finicky tour members with the words, "human
nature."

March 24, Mexico City This was the first day of our tour. As we were
getting onto our bus, street vendors descended on us, hawking machine-
made tablecloths and acrylic serapes. One man was selling little plastic
helicopters. The first one he demonstrated for us settled irretrievably on

the hotel awning; a second one landed on a passing car. The vendor was bewildered by his bad luck but not surprised. Elaine felt sorry for him and, although she had no use for toys, bought two. She also feels sorry for beggars. Roy has told her the Mexican government discourages begging, but when Elaine sees an Indian woman sitting on the pavement with her rag doll baby and her hand outstretched, Elaine cannot resist. She fishes self-consciously about in her wallet, unable to settle on too much or too little, finally thrusting some bills at the Indian woman, who wonders what she is expected to give up for so much money.

As we drove through the city, Elaine was intimidated by the street names—Avenidas Insurgentes and Niños Héroes, Avenida de la Revolución—and by the proliferating monuments, including one to the "Expropriation of the Oil Companies." Since I am a woman and her friend, my reassurances meant little to her. She listened to Roy, who told her it is perfectly safe in Mexico; that revolutions here are all in the past, implying people have come to their senses. "Now what they need to do," he said, "is get on with it." He listed the things that need to be gotten on with: the air conditioning on the bus is either too cold or not cold enough; the hotel doesn't know how to scramble an egg properly and has wasted money installing bidets when the television sets don't work. Roy is longing to run the country and make something of it. Elaine stared at the squatters' shacks on the sides of the hills, the hills that Enrique has told us belong to the government, and tried to believe Roy's assurances.

When we reached the pyramids in Teotihuacán, Fred and I decided to climb to the top and Elaine started up with us. Roy hurried after her, convincing her the high altitude and the heat would be too much for her. She stayed behind with Roy while we climbed, squeezed in the vise of the hot sun and the stingy air, the two-thousand-year-old dust from the pyramids blowing in our eyes. When we reached the temple at the top, panting and exhausted, and looked down on the dwarfed figures below, I understood why they made the pyramids so high: from such a height it would not be difficult for the priests to order the deaths of the dwarfed people beneath them.

March 27, Guanajuato On the way to Guanajuato, Enrique, at Roy's suggestion, had us rotate so everyone had a chance at the front seats in the bus. Roy has an intimidating sense of fairness. He was sitting directly behind Elaine. I saw him lean forward and, gently touching Elaine's shoulder, point out a huddle of cows standing in the highway like guests at the wrong party. Elaine pointed to brightly colored laundry hanging on the trees like huge, ragged blossoms. From our air-conditioned bus we looked out at the dry riverbeds, the horses lying down in the shade, the sun shining on the corrugated iron roofs, farmers and their oxen nearly obscured by plumes of dust. Enrique spoke to us of human nature. "The devil," he said, "is not smart because he is the devil, but because he is old."

Outside Guanajuato the bus stopped beside a cemetery. Some years ago, Enrique told us, it was discovered that because of certain chemicals in the soil, bodies buried there did not decompose. We were invited to view this phenomenon. Dutifully, we got out of the bus and entered a long, narrow, windowless building. We imagined something like the Egyptian mummies, all neatly wrapped in strips of cloth. Instead, we found rows of glass cases filled with bodies in varying stages of arrested decomposition, their skin like leather, their mouths gaping, their eye sockets empty. Some had wisps of hair; a few were completely dressed in dusty black suits or dresses. One man had metal grippers on his shorts, suggesting something much too recent. Elaine ran out of the building and Roy hurried after her. The rest of us remained to file obediently by the cases, pretending polite interest, like courteous dinner guests choking down the remains of a dish in which a roach has been discovered.

I saw that Fred wanted to take my hand, but felt such a gesture would be a confirmation of all we had tried on this trip to put aside. Fred needn't have worried about me; I wasn't as shocked as some of the others. I didn't believe it was the chemicals in the soil that preserved the mummies, but a refusal on their part to moulder away and dissolve, to fall into nothingness. I admired their stubbornness.

When we returned to the bus, Roy was still trying to calm Elaine. It was the first time I had seen her angry. Her face was puckered like a child too obstinate to cry. She was furious with the travel agency, the tour director, the bus driver, with everyone who had led her back to the thing she had meant to escape.

In Guanajuato we went to the Mercado Hidalgo, a market held in a vast, domed building with the hollow echo of a train station. We wandered by stalls heaped with tomatoes, oranges, potatoes, bananas—all arranged so carefully that, in a pile of hundreds of fruits or vegetables, the absence of one or two could be noticed. A small dog, running away from a butcher's stall, held part of a steer's skull between his teeth, the two curved horns protruding from either side of his mouth like huge, ivory mustaches. The brashness of the little dog cheered Elaine, who set about buying back the world. She bought huaraches, wooden beads, an embroidered blouse, and a straw donkey. On our way out of the market, we passed a woman who had nothing more than a dozen empty Coke bottles to sell. They were washed and polished and spread out on the ground in the shape of a fan. Elaine stopped and bought four of the empty bottles. Roy looked pained, as though pity were a kind of giving up, an admission things were as bad as they seemed.

March 29, Pátzcuaro We were taken to the island of Janitzio today. It is advertised in the brochure as a place where fishermen still fish with "butterfly nets." Roy said primitivism and inefficient methods shouldn't be encouraged.

Fred said, "It's only for the tourists."

He was right. As we approached Janitzio, two or three fishing boats took off from the island. When they were nearly alongside of us, the men unfurled their outsized butterfly nets and made a few halfhearted passes at the water. Cameras snapped. After a moment or two, the nets were put away while the fishermen maneuvered their boats close enough to ours to pass their hats. When we reached the island, Fred rather righteously pointed out along the shore the more usual fishing nets strung up on poles.

It was therefore in a spirit of skepticism that we disembarked onto the island. We were wrong. The island was entirely real. There was only a handful of things for sale: postcards, straw hats, and tiny fried fish you would not think worth the eating. The four of us wandered through the island's winding streets. Nearly every house had a pig. At first we thought that was funny and made jokes about the pigs. The joking stopped when we got a look inside the houses—the first time on our trip we had been within touching distance of poverty. The small, square shacks of the fishermen had dirt floors and no windows. When there was furniture, it was nothing more than a bed covered with a soiled blanket or burlap bags. Fred and Elaine and I became more and more silent. Roy was as disturbed as we were, but he was busy with causes and cures: the fishing had probably declined; some other business was needed; the island was located in the middle of a large and scenic lake—why couldn't it be turned into a resort? We said yes, yes, but without conviction. I could see Elaine was upset. She had not planned to travel this far.

A priest in a black cassock emerged from one of the houses and disappeared around a corner. Elaine started after him and in a moment was out of sight. The three of us stood there, uncertain whether we ought to follow her. We had no idea what Elaine wanted of him, but instinctively we felt an approach to a priest ought to be a private occasion.

We walked along slowly, waiting for Elaine to catch up to us. When she didn't return, we thought she might be at the landing waiting for us, but when we reached the pier, she wasn't there. Roy and Fred explained what had happened to Enrique and the three of them set out. Twenty minutes later they were back with a white-faced and shaken Elaine.

On the boat back she told us, "I was upset over what I was seeing. I wanted to give the people something, but I didn't want to hurt their feelings. Then I saw the priest and I thought, I'll give money to him and he'll know who needs it the most. I tried to catch him, but by then he was quite far ahead of me. I didn't want to make myself conspicuous by running, so I lost him. In my hurry I hadn't noticed where I was going, and when I started back to you, I discovered I was lost. Every street I turned into was just like the street I left—the same houses, the same open doorways, and when you looked inside, the same dark, narrow room with its dirt floor and the people standing inside, perfectly still, watching me with no expression on their faces.

"It wasn't just that I was lost, but all my life I've never passed a house without being able to imagine what it would be like to live there—not my life, but theirs. No matter what the house was like, I could see myself moving around inside, working in the kitchen, or standing at the window looking out at myself looking in. I liked the possibility of other lives.

"It was different on the island. However much I tried, I couldn't see myself in those dark rooms, I couldn't imagine any conversations you could have there. I don't think we should have been taken to that island. I don't think it's ready for us."

Since Janitzio, Elaine has been more than ever in Roy's company. I mean she is actually in it, as though she had climbed in. He orders her meals and supervises her shopping: no one could be better cared for, yet I recognize the relinquishment in the way she looks at everything.

I watch on my balcony as Elaine stands at the edge of the ocean. I sense from the way she hastily backs away from the water as the tide moves in, Elaine has decided to marry Roy. She watches the small Mexican boy run at the waves. He shrieks as the surf washes over him, toppling him into the water. He belongs to the beach vendor, who is busy working the hotel guests, making his way among the lounge chairs, holding out dresses in crayon colors of turquoise, pink, and orange. His son becomes increasingly daring. He plunges into the wave as tall as he is. He doesn't reappear. He has lost his footing and the undertow sweeps him out over his head. No one else seems to see this. The vendor has moved on to another chair. The American is taking more pictures of the girl in the bikini. The Mexican family is ordering lunch. I am on a balcony ten stories above the beach. The hotel employs no lifeguards; you are free to drown or not, just as you please.

Elaine has seen. She dives into the water. Seconds later she has the boy. He is shaking his head and spitting. Angrily he pushes Elaine away and, deeply offended at having received help from a woman, runs off toward his father. Probably the boy would have been all right; following his father about each day, he must be used to the ocean. The rescue might have been nothing more than an extravagant gesture, but Elaine believes in what she has done; walking across the beach toward the hotel she has a surprised look on her face, as if she has just realized how much of herself is still left.

This evening, the last night of the tour, there is a farewell dinner on the top floor of our hotel. The restaurant is lit by candles. For the first time we are all dressed up—the women, a little self-conscious in soft dresses and high heels; the men, important in ties and jackets. You can see Roy is thinking how pretty Elaine looks. She turns her head coquettishly toward Roy, and the silver earrings, for which she paid too much, flash and shimmer in the candlelight, but her eyes are thoughtful; she is being giddy out of habit. From the windows we look out at the harbor, where a cruise ship strung with lights lies at anchor. By now our group has acquired a store of family jokes which we trot out. We exchange addresses, reluctant to leave one another, yet we are already moving through our darkened and deserted homes, turning on lights and opening the letters that have been patiently awaiting us.

When dinner is over, Elaine announces she is going to sit on the beach for a while. Roy disapproves, reminding Elaine it is dark and the beaches are for everyone. When he sees she is adamant, he says, "Then I'll go with you."

"No," Elaine tells him, "I want some time by myself. You understand."

He doesn't. "I don't think you should go out there alone."

"I want to," Elaine says, and goes. It is a little revolution to which no one will erect a monument. Loneliness had been forced upon her, but now she chooses it. Fred and I decide to have a nightcap in the bar and invite Roy.

"I can't leave her," Roy says.

"She's left you," I say, not very graciously. Roy tags along with us, talking the waiter into giving us a better table, coaching us on what beer to have. "Cerveza Bohemia," he orders for the three of us. We let him have his way. "I'd like to see this country go bilingual," he says, "like Canada, only Spanish-English. Someone ought to suggest it to them." Fred and I are silent, amazed Roy can believe that understanding is a matter of words. When we get ready to leave, Fred, who has long since mastered the Mexican currency, asks Roy to figure out the bill for him.

This morning, waiting in line at the airport, the tour members are stoic. Apart from relief, rewards at the end of a homeward journey are meager. Roy is speaking with a ticket agent. There is a sweet, satisfied look on Roy's face. He has found a woman who is having trouble with her reservation. After he takes care of this inconvenience for her, it is likely she will have other problems. On the plane trip home, Roy will devote himself to solving them, believing, little by little, he is improving the world.

I think of Elaine the night before on the beach, the waves secretly coaxing onto the shore shells and bits of smooth glass for someone to discover in the morning; the cruise ship slipping its mooring and moving out to sea, its lights mingling haphazardly with the stars; hotel dishwashers and busboys stripping down to their bathing suits and plunging into the cooling water, calling out to one another mild Spanish obscenities that are decently swallowed up by the slamming surf; the faint outline of the cross above Las Brisas that is like the absence of a shadow against a dark wall; and the mountains, which, with no expectations, continue to go about their business.

Elaine is ahead of us in the check-in line, nudging her bags along the floor with a series of small, prodding kicks, the luggage completely under her control. She looks cheerful, though, unlike Roy, not optimistic: they have seen different things.

When Elaine gets home, *Field and Stream* and *Sports Illustrated* will be waiting for her. She might open the magazines and explore their shiny pages, or she might not. While she dusts and vacuums she might turn the radio on to mask the silence in the house, or she might leave the radio off and trail the silence, austere but companionable, along with her. I say goodbye to Elaine; we are boarding different planes.

Fred and I had a letter from the boys saying they will meet us. We will all be relieved to have the trip to talk about.

Two Are Better Than One

Father Jerome Bowman foraged among a row of bottles on his desk for the aspirin and vitamin C. His throat was raw and there was a sharp pain in his chest which might be pleurisy or even pneumonia. He avoided his view from his study window, which had not changed in five months. With the disappearance of fences, boundaries became uncertain; even the ground on which you walked had to be taken on faith. In the scriptures snow was nothing more than a comparative; various things were white as snow: hair or robes or, occasionally, sins. The Lord had never actually let snow *fall* on anything.

If he were to believe with Saint Thomas Aquinas that nature was the mirror of divine perfection, what was he to make of the blank landscape? He closed his eyes to shut out the monotonous whiteness and imagined Aquinas on a bright spring day, striding through the Italian countryside on his way from Rome to the papal court at Orvieto. He would follow the Tiber as it wound through the green countryside. On the distant Alban hills there would be flocks of sheep massed together like low-hanging clouds. Father Bowman wanted to include flowers and birds in his little fantasy, but at that moment they were beyond his imagining.

He picked up his breviary, hoping for one of the more cheering psalms to turn up, as a confirmed slot-machine player looks for a row of oranges or lemons. He didn't want David crying out for the Lord to break the arms of his enemies, or worse, David in one of his whiny, depressed moods. He wanted the psalm in which mountains skip like rams and the hills like lambs or the one where oil runs down Aaron's beard, an image he found endearing.

Father Bowman was a young priest and this was his first parish. The parish was located in a small midwestern town, well to the north of the rest of the world. The town had grown up around the wounding and emptying of the earth. There were deep gouges where ore had been extracted and nearby, in a kind of compensating topography, mounds of tailings. The tailings had formed a scar tissue of soils; if spring came they would appear, deceptively, as green hills.

Father Jerry—for in a futile effort to appear matey with his parishioners it was thus he offered himself—was trying to endure this, his first winter, with grace, stoically shoveling a path from the rectory to the church each morning, and wearing his Irish fisherman's sweater beneath his cassock for weekday Mass, when the small number of participants did not justify the expense of bringing the temperature of the church up to the comfort level. As he read from the Gospel he found a certain wry amusement at seeing his breath emitted in little white puffs, as though out of the chill the Holy Spirit was made manifest.

Father Jerry was fond of his parish, as a child might prize a bird's feather or a pretty stone, knowing that among the many things he could not have—an Arabian horse or a trip to the moon—this at least was his own. He was conscientious in his parish duties, visiting the old and instructing the young. During the summer he had been a competent shortstop on the softball team sponsored by Pizza Galore and had tried to understand why the team did not invite him to accompany them to Steve's Bar after the games. He supposed that even in jeans and an old flannel shirt he emitted sanctimoniousness like some cloying aftershave lotion.

His special project was Harmony House, the aftercare home for patients released from the state mental hospital. When he had found his parishioners writing letters to the editor objecting to having the home in their neighborhood, he had delivered a homily on Paul's admonition that the strong ought to bear the infirmities of the weak. The complaints had gone underground and the house was opened. Since it was his creature, he was regular in his visits. The bedrooms, with their posters and pleasantly cluttered look, suggested a college dorm. With one or two exceptions the residents appeared more normal than he, going to and coming from school and jobs and nodding to him in so offhand and courteous a way that each time he was ready to end his visit, he found himself questioning whether it was he who ought to be leaving. He began to see what the neighbors had feared.

Not all of his efforts bore fruit. When he tried jollying the members of the Altar Society as he recalled the priests of his childhood doing, the women had let him know they took their fairs and rummage sales seriously and had retaliated by trying to bully him into allowing altar girls, even though they knew the bishop had forbidden it. His sugges-tion to the parish council that they buy a computer (his seminary had offered a course in business machines) was quickly turned down: "Next thing, you'll want a robot to say Mass for us, Father." A humble man, Father Jerry accepted, even agreed with these little corrections.

He told himself he had not had time to earn the devotion of his parish, that he ought not even expect it. It was their devotion to the Lord that mattered. Still, he was disappointed when dinner invitations were scarce and took to reading Merton on the desert fathers, relishing the thought of blazing sun and scorching sand. He had once considered entering a monastery but had chosen parish life as the more grati-fying vocation, picturing himself as the esteemed head of a devoted family. Now he saw he was to be a solitary without the consolation of a brotherhood.

In March, with the snow still coming down and the temperature remaining at zero, tempers had become short and unpleasantness erupted in the parish council over the iron stakes in the church ceme-tery. Long ago the forest of stakes had been pounded into place to mark grave lot boundaries when snow lay three feet deep. Now the church had the amenity of a holding shed where bodies were tucked away until the ground thawed receptively in the spring. There was no longer a need to plunge beneath the snow and hack at the frozen ground. The majority of the congregation wanted the stakes removed, claiming the cemetery looked like a vampires' burial ground. Pro-stakers, the older men who had hammered in the markers, did not like their work going for nothing.

Fewer people were turning up in the room of reconciliation during Lenten confessions to chat face-to-face about a tendency to gossip or an impatience with their spouses and children, mild sins that were so innocuous as to be a boast. Instead, the parishioners were choosing the anonymity of the grill to admit shameful indiscretions. The whole congregation appeared to be working its way down through the Ten Commandments and were now well into the raunchy stuff. Alarmed, Father Jerry sounded out Father Richard, whose parish he had visited while assisting at a penance service, and was told the slippage was an annual event. "It's the weather," Father Richard reassured him, "People just naturally want to get into a warm bed and snuggle up. This time of year one bed's as good as another."

Father Jerry was wondering if he could afford to heat the church basement an evening or two a week to give his parishioners some wholesome amusement—movies, perhaps, or a marriage encounter session, although it might not be the proper time for the latter—when God had touched Father Jerry, as he had touched Job, in his person. Father Jerry developed a sore throat, a headache, stomach cramps, and the full complement of gastrointestinal symptoms. He had felt so miserable he had called Harmony House to cancel his weekly visit. He could not face the prospect of leaving the warmth of the rectory. On his brief passage to the church that morning, the wind howling in from the open spaces of western Canada had nearly knocked him over. What he longed to do was go upstairs and fall into bed, but someone might come for a Mass card or to pay their pledge on the roof repairs. It would not do for him to appear at the door in a bathrobe, particularly as his robe was not a conservative brown or gray—even a priest could not be expected to wear a black bathrobe—but a red plaid given to him by a light-minded aunt when he entered the seminary. Recalling the aunt, who used to stuff him with candy forbidden by his parents, he realized it was not just the comfort of a bed that he wished for, but a sympathizing presence which might be mother or sister or aunt; but whatever it was, it was disconcertingly feminine.

Father Jerry had been one of those precocious children addicted to books, a child who from his earliest years went eagerly to school and sat down to his homework as to a feast. His mother rejoiced but his father rushed him out onto the ball field. The boy had seen where the power lay and dutifully learned to move in on the ground balls and fade back for the slowly arching flies. Occasionally he would allow himself a lapse—a day home from school when he was only slightly under the weather. His mother would fuss over him as though he were a warrior back from some cruel and distant battle. Now she was far away with his father, who had retired and taken her to live in South Carolina. Their condominium had two bedrooms, but his father had turned the extra one into a workshop where he carved decoys to supplement his pension. On the rare occasions when Father Jerry visited, he had to sleep on the living-room couch. His father had chronic insomnia, and Father Jerry would be awakened in the middle of the night by the biting and scraping of a chisel as his dad shaped a block of wood to his liking, giving Father Jerry an uncomfortable sense of déjà vu.

In times past there had been housekeepers to bustle about rectories, cleaning and cooking, alternately chivying and spoiling their priests. The coming together of austerity and egalitarianism in the church had put an end to all that. In Father Jerry's diocese priests took their cue from the bishop, who made his own bed and cooked his own meals. It was not unusual for the bishop to include a thrifty recipe or two in his dispatches on financial crises. At gatherings of the diocesan priests, conversation turned to electric woks and Stouffer's lasagne.

Deprived of their housekeepers, rectories became overquiet. Although this void was never spoken of openly among the priests, who preferred to profess pleasure at having their quarters to themselves, nevertheless increasing numbers of rectories were harboring golden retrievers and labradors.

Father Jerry thought enviously of Father Richard's gift for making friends. He was followed about by small smiling children who brought him their pets to baptize. The parents of the children entertained Father Richard at tables laden with roast turkeys and hams, home-baked biscuits and thickly frosted chocolate cakes. His altar swarmed with lectors and special ministers of the Eucharist. When it came time for the exchange of peace, Father Richard was up and down the church aisles pressing flesh, the white rubber soles of his topsiders flashing out from under his cassock.

Father Jerry was saved further spiteful thoughts by the ringing of his doorbell. His chest was worse and his sweater no longer warmed him. He would have liked to ignore the bell, but perhaps someone was dying and he was wanted to administer the Sacrament of the Sick. The pleasant expectation of being needed gave him the strength to drag himself to the door. Last week two young men, neatly dressed in suits as black as his, had appeared on his doorstep and tried to convert him to another faith. He could see in their eyes the excitement of the fisherman who has sighted the biggest trout of them all. Rather mischievously, he allowed them to play him a bit before he began to recruit *them*. They fled as before the devil incarnate.

He opened the door to admit Anna Beasly. Her grizzled fake-fur coat and knitted tam were covered with snow. She wore men's work gloves, wool stockings whose lumps and wrinkles gave away the untidy long underwear that lurked beneath them, and galoshes. Her gray hair stuck out of the tam in wisps and her face, covered with several days' accumulation of powder and lipstick, had the appearance of a kabuki player's. As she brushed past him, there was the musty smell of damp basements.

He had met Anna during his first visit to Harmony House. She had gone up to him at once, as though she had been waiting for him, and by a series of surreptitious and bizarre signals had indicated she had something to show him. He had consulted the house manager, who explained, "She's got a craft downstairs she's doing." Plucking at his sleeve and dancing along in front of him, Anna had led him to the basement. There she turned on a switch to reveal one entire wall covered by a mural painted in garish colors. Against a background of blue mountains and red sea were figures dressed in what he supposed was meant to be biblical garb. There were Adam and Eve exchanging accusing looks beneath an apple tree, Noah and his sons arranged like a family portrait, a smug Joshua in front of the crumbling walls of Jericho. It was the faces that caught Father Jerry's attention. The background and the bodies were painted, but the faces themselves had been cut from newspaper photographs. Adam was a former secretary of state; Eve, the anchor on a morning news show; Noah, a consumer advocate; and his sons, a rock group. This was unsettling. Father Jerry secretly felt that inhabitants of the Old Testament with their recidivism were an embarrassment. He wanted them firmly pressed between the covers of the Bible and not resurrected as familiars.

Anna began to drop by the rectory, a shoebox of clippings under her arm. She covered his desk with photographs of former presidents, cor-

poration officers, the winner of the state lottery, a boxing champion.
What did he think about Arnold Schwarzenegger as Goliath and Woody
Allen as David? When her visits became too frequent, Father Jerry
approached the social worker at Harmony House to see if Anna's medication might be stepped up. In the days before medication, he knew she
would have been one of the back-ward patients, frozen to a chair, gazing fixedly at the middle distance, arrested by some disconcerting inner
vision. Her psychiatrist was called. He said no. It appeared that larger
doses made Anna break out in a rash. Father Jerry got the impression
that for some people, too much sanity was risky.

Now here she was, just when he least wanted to see her. He resisted
an impulse to push her back through the door, stopped by the fear that
his hands would go right through her, for there was something ecto-
plasmic about her, suggesting she could exercise options like going
up in a puff of smoke. Her yellow eyes examined him and she said,
"When you canceled Harmony House today, I knew you must be sick.
You look terrible."

Unexpectedly, he was grateful to her. It was reassuring to know the
external signs of his misery were there for the rest of the world to see.
He felt exonerated. She headed for the kitchen, where she looked about
her like a prospective tenant. Although it was ludicrous to think Anna
would be fastidious, Father Jerry winced at the sight of the unwashed
dishes from last night's dinner and this morning's skimpy breakfast of
toast and health-store peanut butter.

"You get some rest," she said. "I'll be right back." She wrapped
herself in her musty odors and vanished through the door.

With even this slight permission, he stumbled upstairs and collapsed
onto his bed. His eyes burned. His head throbbed. He thought long-
ingly of the glasses of freshly squeezed orange juice and the bowls of
rich broth his mother had carried to his sickroom when he was a child.
In the afternoon when her work was done, his mother, having changed
into something fresh and attractive, would tell him stories in which
small, voluble animals had harrowing adventures that ended happily.

When he awoke, his body was shaking with chills. As he pulled up
his blanket, he heard the front door open. Anna had returned. He was
quiet, hoping she might go away, but instead of the longed-for sounds
of departure, he heard the opening and shutting of kitchen cabinets.

The noises increased; Anna loose in his kitchen sounded like a bird trapped in a house—careening against walls in its frenzy, upsetting everything it touched. The noise grew excessive as though there were more than one person. Half-asleep he imagined Anna assisted by the figures in her mural, their long robes scattering the toast crumbs on the kitchen floor, their sandals slipping on globs of peanut butter. They were helping Anna to concoct exotic dishes: blackbird pie, messes of pottage, perhaps, he thought feverishly, a manna quiche. He drifted off to a troubled sleep. When he awoke, the afternoon sun had reached his window so that the room was dense with the dots and dashes of motes and rays.

A grinning Anna was standing triumphantly at his door. She had removed her fake-fur coat, but the tam remained. There was a soiled towel tucked into the waist band of her skirt. In her hands she held a baking sheet on which some dishes had been arranged. Food odors, not entirely unpleasant, drifted over to him. "This will fix you up," she told him, lowering the tray onto the lap he had made by hastily sitting up, instinct having warned him he must be alert in her presence—he believed her powers were considerable, for here she was against his will, firmly entrenched in his rectory.

By way of refinement she had spread the baking sheet with a square of paper toweling. He was relieved to find there were no blackbirds screeching to break out of a crust. Instead, resting on the toweling was a bowl of soup in which bits of vegetable and barley floated. There were crackers, a glass of milk, and some rather oddly shaped cookies, obviously homemade. He lifted a spoonful cautiously to his mouth and found the soup good.

Anna settled into his rocking chair and watched rapturously while he ate. "I worked in the kitchen at the state hospital," she said. "I was salad cook. Coleslaw. Week in and week out. That's all they got with their dinner until I took over. I'll tell you a little story about that." She crossed one bumpy leg over the other and folded her arms across her chest. She was rocking back and forth a little too rapidly. It made Father Jerry dizzy. He closed his eyes and, sinking into his pillows, waited like a child to be told a story.

"We had these psychiatrists come out to the hospital," she said. "Research people. Stuck us with needles, and every morning we had to pee in little paper cups. Well, we heard they found out what made us crazy—some chemical in what we put in the little paper cups. People on the outside who weren't crazy didn't have nearly so much of the chemical. So the research people got all excited.

"Well, just about then was when I moved from dishwasher to salad cook and I could never stand coleslaw; you might as well chew wet sawdust. I switched to head lettuce cut up with tomatoes and radishes and green pepper and got a lot of compliments. But the research doctors were having a fit because all the chemicals had disappeared. They came down to the kitchen wanting to know if our diet had changed any. The dietician told them about how we weren't getting the coleslaw anymore. Next day their faces were right down to the floor. It seems the chemical they thought was a crazy chemical was just a cabbage chemical." Anna burst into shrieks of laughter, seesawing back and forth in the rocker with so much vigor, the rocker began to lurch forward like a large, awkward bird for whom flight is not quite possible.

Father Jerry smiled. The food had done him good. From his bed he could look out of his window. The ground was not visible so he did not have to contemplate the besetting snow. Although it was nearly six in the evening, the sky was still light; spring was coming on. There might be many of these chats with Anna. He saw choice was an extravagance he would not be able to afford. He could not say he minded. He experienced a kind of peace in surrender. He had felt something similar as a child sleeping at night in the back seat of the family car while his father drove and his mother watched. He was shut into the world, traveling through darkness, and glad enough not to be alone.

The Showing

Hunting for mushrooms, Agnes Dillon kept up a little counterpoint of prayer that she would not come upon one of her husband's traps. It was sure to have in it a small corpse—a bog lemming or a meadow vole, a shrew or a mole or a white-footed mouse. She never knew so kind a man to wreak such havoc. Since Keith's retirement to the north woods after years of teaching biology at the state university, he had fought the idea that his productive days were over by launching, in a frenzy of research, one experiment after another. The snap traps, fifty of them, were set out in grids each night to determine something called "territorial invasiveness." Agnes wished the attractive little rodents had the sense to stay at home.

It was early May. There were still a few white rags of snow on the north-facing slopes of the hills. The undecided spring breezes blew warm and cold. In the bright spring light, the blankness of the leafless trees gave an empty look to the woods. The patches of violets, in Easter colors of purple and yellow, were like bouquets of flowers set about an unfurnished room.

Agnes entered the woods of their neighbor, Mr. Selkirk, who appeared only during deer-hunting season, when his enthusiasm and poor marksmanship confined Agnes and Keith to their cabin. Since Mr. Selkirk's land was not his to tamper with, Keith seldom went there. Agnes went often, hoping her repeated presence would send Mr. Selkirk's deer elsewhere.

As she bent to pick a little huddle of morels, her knees cracked and the binoculars strung around her neck thumped heavily against her chest. Close to the earth she could smell the rank odor of wild leek. The morels were cool and damp in her hand. A red spider scurried through the convolutions of one of them. She shook the spider gently onto the ground and dropped the morels in a spring bag. As she carried the bag along, the spores from the gathered mushrooms would scatter productively over the earth.

There was a shuffling of dry leaves. Peering through the binoculars, she saw a bird with an olive-brown back and pink legs. She was pleased. You often heard ovenbirds nattering at you from the hidden depths of a tree but you seldom saw them. She hoped it would stay where it was. Keith had left their cabin at five that morning, weighed down with yards of mist netting. He was banding birds, anxious to get his hands on the little migrating warblers.

Looking up, Agnes saw what she thought was a mourning dove. She raised her binoculars. Mourning doves usually kept to town backyards. It was certainly the right shape—the ball-like body, the sharply pointed tail, the neck and head that formed a hook—but the bird was too large, and the color wrong; instead of a pale mauve gray, its back was slate, and its chest reddish. She knew the name of the bird, but was afraid to say it. In a moment it would fly away and she could pretend it had never been there.

Perversely, the bird remained perched on the tree, its color bright against the dark green of the hemlock. It was a passenger pigeon. Yet that was impossible. The last one had died seventy years ago, a pitiful captive in some zoo. Passenger pigeons once surged through the sky like great feathered rivers; then their nesting grounds, the forests of pine and birch, were cut down. The pigeons were killed and sold by the millions to fancy restaurants. Even the squabs were snatched from their nests. Finally, disease had come along to trouble them, and the passenger pigeon, besieged on every side, had disappeared from the face of the earth.

As Agnes watched, the pigeon flew off. She sank down on a patch of moss and listened to the knocking of her heart. She felt she had been picked up bodily and shaken, but she did not doubt. Since there was so much that was not known, she believed anything was possible. On her morning walks she had discovered holes in the ground, tunnels across the road, a pile of feathers—things that had gone on while she wasn't watching. For thirty years she had wondered how the birch bark she found scattered about in the woods was pulled from the trees; then one day she saw the wind unwind a swath of bark as though it were a bandage. You could probe and dissect all you liked, but the important thing was to be there. Perhaps there were many passenger pigeons, but until now, no one had been there to see them.

Keith would be astonished when she told him, but she made no move in the direction of their cabin. Last year an eagle had flown over their pond. She watched it grazing the tops of the trees and marveled at how much of the sky the bird took up. She told Keith, who, full of excitement, had called several colleagues. Fanning out through the woods, they had found the hodgepodge of the eagle's nest at the top of a pine tree. At once they set up an observation platform in a large maple near the nest. The men were possessive and secretive like boys building a tree house. They believed that because of their research, eagles everywhere would be better off. They were against ignorance, even mystery. Between them they manned the platform twenty-four hours a day. The second week of the encampment, the harassed eagles abandoned their young and were never seen again.

Keith waved to her from the other side of the pond. He was a slight and agile man and looked engagingly boyish. He had stretched his net between two oaks. As she drew closer she could see, fluttering in the interstices of the net, small brown-and-yellow birds struggling to free themselves. Keith gently untangled a warbler from the netting and clamped a band around its leg. The bird, stricken, lay for a moment in Keith's hand, and then, seeing its chance, flew off. "Aggie, dear, look here, a chestnut-sided warbler. We haven't had one in a couple of years." His face went sweet with pleasure.

"But it's dead," Agnes said. The diminutive brown-and-rust bird lay imprisoned in the net, its neck awkwardly twisted.

"Yes. It's a pity." He regarded Agnes more closely. "You look flushed." He laid his hand gently on her forehead. "Warm. Better go in the house and have a rest. I'll fix us a nice morel omelet as soon as I finish here."

Entering the house, Agnes was confounded by the familiarity of their living room: the rugs faintly soiled along the usual paths from one known room to another, the residual smell of Keith's pipe, the ticking

of the grandfather clock Keith had spent months making for her. Everything conspired to turn the passenger pigeon into an illusion. As always, the familiar overpowered the unfamiliar. She wondered how the
saints clung to their visions.

Agnes, thinking of the birds struggling in the net, kept her secret
through dinner. As usual, she knitted while they watched the evening
television news; knitting seemed to give the disorderly events a sense of
tidiness. Could she possibly keep from Keith the ornithological happening of the century? He would report the bird, of course; it would
make his reputation. His picture would appear in all the papers, perhaps on television as well. She looked suspiciously at the screen, remembering the rare shore bird that had been reported on the east coast
a few years before. The networks had shown it hopping along the sand,
surrounded by hundreds of bird fanciers who had flown in from all over
the country, greedy to add the accidental to their life lists. In the face of
so many people, the passenger pigeon would desert its nest, and any
chance of its multiplying would be lost. Still, Agnes thought, it might
be that she could win Keith over to secrecy.

"Do you remember," she asked him, "when we were in that red-
woods park in California and we saw the quote from Walt Whitman?"
There had been a display explaining the history of the redwood trees.
The legends on the signs were terse and factual, but the last one was
the Whitman quote: "You must not know too much or be too precise or
scientific about birds and trees and flowers; a certain vagueness—
perhaps ignorance, credulity—helps your enjoyment of these things."

"I suppose by now his boss has seen the sign and given whoever put
it up the heave-ho," Keith said. "A scientific display is no place for
romance."

"I don't think he was being romantic," Agnes told him. "He was
talking about mystery."

"Same thing." He handed her a journal, open to a picture of a hawk
wrapped in leather straps. "Just look at that transmitter harness. If we
did that with our hawks, we could find exactly where they're nesting.
All you would need is a mobile tracking unit and a portable receiver."

"What if they don't want you to know?" she asked.

"Animals are not creatures from the pages of *Winnie the Pooh*,"

Keith said. "They don't think about things. They just are. Besides, the population of the rough-legged hawks has been going down. We need to know why."

At this she fell silent, for not long ago the number of robins began to dwindle. By banding the flocks that remained, Keith had learned the robins that had fallen off were the ones digging for worms in nearby potato fields. His discovery led to the banning of a pesticide. Now the robins were back in force. What had she, with all her sentimentality, done for those robins?

In bed that night she could feel Keith's reassuring warmth just inches away. It was hard to imagine him keeping a secret from her, or even having one. She considered her silence a deception and felt guilty. She did not know why she had been chosen to see the passenger pigeon. Her life seemed so ordinary: housework, walks in the woods, her daughter and the grandchildren. There had been days when she worried that the Lord had not noticed her in all that uneventful sameness. She had found herself wishing something exceptional would happen to her. This desire had frightened her, for she feared being pushed forward into the world, where visibility would make her vulnerable. She knew there was safety in her inconsequence. Still, she had thought there must be more to life, or at the very least, she had not counted correctly everything she had. Now her singularity distressed her.

In the morning Keith emptied the refrigerator of several dead birds, fatalities of his previous day's netting, and took them off to prepare. It was a delicate skill which Keith practiced well. He had drawers full of little feathered shells of various unthinking birds. When she held the skins in her hand, Agnes was overcome by their emptiness.

Out-of-doors Agnes was glad to enter a world where things grew and moved. Reluctantly she breathed the spiderwebs stretched across her path—someone's work gone for nothing. She scanned first one tree and then another, hastily at first and then slowly and more carefully. This time it was a beech tree. She followed the creased, wrinkled gray trunk two-thirds of the way up and found the pigeon shifting restlessly from branch to branch. After a while the bird flew off to a farther tree. When she followed, it moved farther still, and finally was gone, releasing her. She told herself that if she were to keep her secret, she ought to find out if there were going to be more passenger pigeons. Each time she saw the bird she must mark the direction of its flight to help her locate the nest.

It was a pity she could not ask for Keith's help. He was experienced at finding the nests of birds and wrote expert papers on their location, on the number of eggs, and when the bird fledged. The papers carried a caveat explaining the mortality rate of the nests he observed was apt to be high, since a fox or raccoon sometimes followed his scent. She decided not to search out the possible nest of the passenger pigeon.

Agnes began to rise early. Each morning she went out to confront the bird. That was how she thought of the witnessing of its appearance. If *it* were there, then *she* must be there; it was the least or the most she could do. She saw it on dull days, when its red chest seemed merely rufous, and on bright days, when its breast, touched by the sun, glowed brightly. By early June it was flying off with insects in its mouth. Carrying them to its young? In her excitement she could almost imagine how delicious the crisp green bugs might taste.

A morning late in June came when the passenger pigeon was not there. A white-throated sparrow sang. A flock of cedar waxwings with their black bandit masks stole from a Juneberry bush. Any other day these sights would have been enough. If something had happened to the pigeon, she accused herself, it would be her fault. As soon as someone gave you a gift, you were responsible for it. Agnes stayed in the woods all day searching for the bird, going without breakfast or lunch, returning home weak and shaky in time to make dinner, so Keith would not be suspicious. Luckily, he was occupied with a loon he had caught in one of the floating bail traps he set out for ducks. He had been wanting to band the loon for some time, but the loon was seclusive. Agnes had once seen it on a remote lake where it had gone to molt. Hundreds of its curled breast feathers had blown over the surface of the lake, coming to rest on the water like fanciful barques. Since the loon could not escape into flight during its molting period, she had neglected at the time to say anything to Keith.

The next day the pigeon was back. Twice that week she missed it. She began to attend daily Mass, appealing to a higher authority to tell her what to do about the pigeon. In those early morning hours, even close friends slipped in and out of the church without a word to one

another, their evasive, conspiratorial looks and cryptic smiles acknowledging the trials that lay behind so fervent a devotional practice. Although Agnes was regular, no answer came down.

In August Agnes and Keith's daughter, Carol, and Carol's husband,
Robert, came to spend a week, bringing with them their sons, eight-
year-old Blake and six-year-old Terry. The grass had faded to a gray-
brown, and along the roadside you could see, in the first red leaves, a
harbinger of fall. A cold rain began to fall and would not stop. Keith
built fires to keep the damp out of the house. They stayed inside and
played five-hundred rummy and watched old westerns on TV. Locked
in the house together for days, Agnes felt their edges dissolve and
meld. Occasionally one of them would disappear into a bedroom to
write letters or read, but in minutes they would be back to look out of
the window with the others, as though the storms were a command
performance. Only Terry kept to himself. He filled the bathtub with
pillows and, closing the shower curtain, used the bath sponge to paste
stickers in a notebook.

Agnes never stopped thinking of the passenger pigeon, worrying that
the unseasonable weather might send it precipitously south. She had
already sighted an early flock of snow buntings, a sure sign of fall,
their white wings fluttering in the air like the blizzards to come.

On the last day of the visit, they awoke to find the walls of their
bedrooms kindled by the sun. Carol said at breakfast she felt light and
might at any moment float off her chair. They planned a picnic for the
afternoon. Keith and Robert went off to dismantle a beaver lodge to see
what means the beavers used to protect themselves from invaders. The
boys were invited but only Blake went along. Terry looked unhappy at
the idea, asking "Why do you want to wreck their house?" Carol
suggested she and Agnes pick blackberries for jam.

"They'll be too full of water to cook up properly," Agnes said. "I
think I'll go for a little walk. Terry, do you want to come along?" The
boy followed her outside.

Everything glittered in the new sun. The wet tree trunks were slick
black glass. On the leaves, drops of water flashed white and gold.
Agnes pointed out a hawk working its wings, climbing higher and
higher, like a child pumping a swing. Terry paid polite attention. Unlike her older, more boisterous grandchild, Terry was reflective. Hours

after you told him something, he would ask a question that showed he had been examining what you said, as he might inspect a shiny beetle to see if it were the biting kind.

When they reached Mr. Selkirk's woods, Agnes cautioned the boy to be still. "We're waiting for something," she said. He accepted her words and worked at trying to see what his grandmother was looking for. When the passenger pigeon appeared in a nearby beech tree, Terry responded to her excited signal. "There," she whispered, pointing, "there on the branch. Do you see it?"

The boy nodded, satisfied.

She told him how the passenger pigeons had ranged over the forests of North America; how the last great nesting of the birds had been only a few miles from where she and Terry were sitting; how their numbers were once so great the branches on which they roosted would break under their weight; how the flocks, passing overhead, would eclipse the light of the sun; how they sounded like a great wind rushing by; how the birds were unafraid of people and would hover about them, lighting on their shoulders and arms; how people followed the birds with clubs and nets and destroyed them.

When the bird flew away, Terry frowned. "You must not tell anyone what you saw," Agnes warned him. He nodded. She did not think he would say anything. If he did, she would explain she had been telling him the story of the passenger pigeon, and his imagination carried him away.

Showing the pigeon to Terry had been a relief. The loneliness of the solitary witness was gone. Still, she regretted having to keep a secret from Keith. Perhaps it was this regret that stopped her from diverting Keith when he suggested a walk in Mr. Selkirk's woods; with the children's departure they had found the house ghostly. Keith had his butterfly net. "There used to be some *polyxenes asterius* over there," he said. "I might take a few home and breed them." He seldom went outside without a purpose.

The summer's last flowers were blooming. As they walked along, Keith recited their Latin names: *Hesperis matronalis, Geranium pratense, Daucus carota, Pyrolaceae.* Agnes felt he was casting a spell. She stepped along beside him, silently giving their real names back: dame's rocket, cranesbill, Queen Anne's lace, Indianpipe.

Keith was searching among the white tracery of wild carrot for swallowtails. Had she remained quiet he might have missed it, but in spite of herself she cried out, "Keith, it's the passenger pigeon!" She longed to share her gift.

Startled, he looked up. There in the beech tree was the bird, its head tilted slightly sidewise, its chest ruby in the sun. "Mourning dove," he said absently, picking apart an oak gall to get at the curled white wasp larva inside.

"Keith, *look* at it. I've watched it all summer. It *is* a passenger pigeon." She couldn't bear his indifference.

He turned away from the bird. "Aggie, you're a hopeless romantic. *Helenium autumnale*," he intoned, "*Mitchella repens, Lychnis coronaria.*"

For a moment his doubt was catching. Then, feeling a great sorrow for him, she slipped her hand in his. "Goldenrod," she urged gently, "sneezeweed, blazing star."

The Secret Meeting with Mr. Eliot

Dear Professor Wally,

   This is not a poem about a cat. It is my life. I graduated from high
school during the height (depth?) of the Depression. Three students in my
class went on to college. Although I was valedictorian (Latin: *valedictus,*
bidden goodbye) and spoke on "The Promise of the Future," I was not one
of them.

   An excellent seamstress, even at that early age, I was fortunate to find a
position in the yard-goods department of a large store where I worked as a
sales*woman* (I will not neuter myself for any movement). I enjoyed my
job. When a customer held a pattern in one hand and a bolt of material
in the other, it was a moment full of possibilities. I seldom had to see
the finished product, which likely had poorly set-in sleeves and an
uneven hemline.

   Apart from a brief leave when the children were small, I worked there
for twenty-eight years. In those days women were not promoted. When I
retired, I was still a saleswoman, while the buyer was a girl of twenty-
three, a management trainee who couldn't tell a tailor tack from a flat
fell seam.

   My husband, Ned, also retired, was an insurance salesman, and while
he was a good provider, there wasn't a whole lot left over. I worked so our
three children could go to college. I have always believed in education and
made it a point to keep up with the children's studies. By working with my
daughter on her French, I learned enough to acquit myself quite creditably
when Ned took me to a very expensive restaurant for our thirtieth wedding
anniversary. Ned was proud of me although he had a little laugh when I
ordered *choucroute* when what I meant was *chou-fleur.* Instead of cauli-
flower, we got sauerkraut, which neither of us likes.

All three of our children graduated from college, none, I'm sorry to say, from The Great University (which is how I think of this place). I shared as much of their college years as I could, making attractive bedspreads and draperies for their college rooms and reading many of their textbooks. All of this is leading up to your course on Mr. Eliot's poetry. Usually I don't care for advanced things like modern art with its blots and squibbles or modern music that sounds to me like a chorus of rasping blue jays, but when one of my daughters brought home Mr. Eliot's poems to read for an English literature course, I took to him at once. I felt he was able to call by name all the vague things I had put out of my mind as too puzzling or too sad. Also, I admire his way with words. I once read the dictionary (collegiate, not the big one) straight through, two pages a night, for a year and a half. Ned said I was out of my head, but I found knowing where words come from most informative.

When I saw in a Senior Learners' bulletin at the library that there was to be a class in Mr. Eliot, I decided I would go. The meaning of his poems moves only inches over my head and I hoped your class would bring it within reach.

Of course, I was also excited at the idea of being on the campus of The Great University and going to classes just like a real student—though it would only be for a week. Also, I had never been away from home by myself, except for the time I spent with my sister, Connie, when she had a cancer operation (successful!!!).

You can imagine my disappointment, then, over what is happening in your course. Or perhaps I should say, *not* happening. I hope you don't mind my being frank with you. I don't think Mr. Eliot is just a laughing matter as you seem to, and I never was afraid of him.

Respectfully,

Dorothy Louise Hillard

In the beginning, The Great University was much as I had hoped. My roommate in the dormitory (Latin: *dormire,* to sleep), whose name was Irene—she was born in Canada and you pronounce the last "e"— was tidy, keeping her possessions on her side of the room. She had a nice little sense of humor, too, and we found ourselves giggling over the way we dressed up just to go down the hall to the lavatory, for all fifteen of the Senior Learners were staying on our floor, including the married couple and an unattached man, Drew (Germanic: loved one) Norton. We thanked the Lord the bathrooms were designated "Men" and "Women," although the signs were printed on cardboard and we suspected they were temporary. What can boys and girls be thinking of these days?

It turned out Irene had insomnia, and when I awakened during that first evening, I could see in the glow of a nightlight, which had been placed in each dorm room for the convenience of the Senior Learners, that Irene was wide awake, a small transistor plugged like a life-support system to her ear. I thought of Mr. Eliot's "anxious worried women" and how they lay awake "trying to unweave, unwind, unravel."

At first I wasn't going to say anything, but my daughter had told me how she would stay up until all hours having chummy talks with her roommate, so I suggested to Irene we put on our robes and slippers and go down to the snack kitchen at the end of the hall for milk and cookies. I am not gregarious by nature and Irene confessed she was not either, but we had much to say to one another, as is often the way when two quiet people find themselves alone in one another's company.

Irene told me she had just lost her husband. I have always thought "lost" an inappropriate word in such cases, with its connotation of negligence. "Nothing works in the house anymore," she said. "The light switch is broken, the bathroom faucet leaks, and the front door has a crack in it. Everything is coming to pieces." I felt very lucky; while Ned would not come to the Senior Learners week with me and only reads the newspapers and *Sports Afield,* he is quite handy and everything in our house works.

However, Irene's husband had been a dentist, and through the years they had attended meetings in New York and San Francisco and even the Caribbean, while Ned's insurance company met in places like Buffalo and Toledo, which are nice, I'm sure, but not that different from the city in which I've lived all my life.

Well, one subject led to another and it was nearly dawn before we got to bed, which made us feel quite sophisticated.

The next morning, waiting for Irene to finish dressing so we could go down to breakfast together, I stood looking out of the window. The whole campus was in leaf. A path led across a wide stretch of lawn and under tall trees to old buildings of brick and newer ones of marble. Lit by the July sun, the red brick glowed and the white marble shimmered.

The campus that summer morning appeared to me a mirage that would surely disappear as I tried to approach it.

An hour later the fifteen of us were actually walking across that very path on the way to our first class: "Why Weeds Are Our Friends." Our second class was "Economic Theory and Your Checkbook." The last course, the one for which I had come, "Meet Mr. Eliot," would be held after lunch.

"We must look like trippers from a nursing home or a mental hospital," I said to Irene. That was unfair. There was nothing decrepit (Latin: *decrepitus*, broken down) about us. Drew Norton had been out jogging that morning and Al and Betty Pinkston, a retired school principal and his wife from South Bend, had played a set of tennis before breakfast. I felt rather proud of the way everyone looked—the men in sport shirts and well-pressed khaki trousers, the women in neat shirt-waist dresses or wash-and-wear slacks and blouses. Edna Blodgett, who reminded me of my gym teacher in fifth grade, had brought her bicycle and was leading the way. Edna wore a nifty split skirt which I knew she had made herself for I recognized the Vogue pattern. Unfortunately, she had bungled her placket so the zipper flashed out at you like a set of metal teeth.

By the time we sat through our two morning classes—sharing memories of weeds we had known and telling more than we might have wished about our financial picture (generally dismal) to the inquisitive economics professor—and had shared a lunch in the dorm cafeteria (where the food was surprisingly tasty if a bit overboard on the cottage-cheese, grated-carrot side), we had established a camaraderie. Chatting away in the classroom waiting for the professor, it seemed we had known one another for years. "Drew," Al Pinkston said, "don't think we didn't guess who switched the signs on the lavatories after lunch." We all laughed.

"I'm not admitting anything," Drew said. "I'll tell you one thing, though. I'm going to start answering back that economics fellow. Tying wages and prices together went out with Marx." He was definitely more attractive in clothes than scanty running shorts, which showed his skinny white legs.

"Well, we're here to listen and learn; then we can make up our own minds." Eve Prill had taken on the role of conciliator (Latin: *conciliatus*, bring together). You had the feeling her life had been spent calming down a hotheaded husband.

"Where did the Mayhews go?" Irene asked.

"They're not taking the Eliot class," Betty Pinkston told her. "They said it would be over their heads. They're going around to used bookstores; he collects old paperback mysteries."

In the other classes I had taken a seat toward the back, less interested in the course itself than the fact that I was there in one of the classrooms of The Great University. For Mr. Eliot I sat in the first row. Lying on my desk was a list of questions I intended to ask, about the footnotes to "The Waste Land." But most of all I just wanted to hear another human being talk out loud about Mr. Eliot.

Our professor arrived in jeans and a blue oxford-cloth shirt with a missing button and pen marks all over the pocket. He was plump with a curly beard and round red cheeks. His hair was shoulder length. I was disappointed. I believe I wanted Mr. Eliot himself to walk in, wearing a bowler and a dark suit and carrying a black umbrella. I did not see how anyone who was plump could satisfactorily explicate (Latin: *explicatus*, unfold) Mr. Eliot.

"Good afternoon," he said. "I'm Professor Wallace Overton, but we aren't going to be formal. We're here for a little fun. Just call me Professor Wally."

I winced. I like a certain amount of tiptoeing around people. I hate it when the new priest says, "Just call me Father Bob," or the nurse in the doctor's office, who is about forty years younger than I, pokes her head into the waiting room and shouts out, "Dorothy."

Professor Wally settled on a corner of the desk, his buttocks oozing like bread dough over the edge. There was the obligatory reciting of names, during which time I kept my eyes fastened on *The Collected Poems,* which he had taken out of his briefcase and laid on the desk beside him.

"So you're here to learn something about T. S. Eliot?" His tone suggested we had come for some faintly obscene reason and there was an embarrassed giggle. "Well, I know you're on vacation so I have no intention of scaring you off with a lot of heavy stuff. I've had a little vacation myself recently. Amy and I spent the month of June in England. In fact, our slides just came back. If you twist my arm, I'll bring them tomorrow." I was distressed to hear a general murmur of approval from the class. Perhaps he noticed my frown for he said, "England, after all, was the country Eliot lived in most of his life, right?

"Let me give any of you planning to go to England a little tip: bed and breakfast is the way to go." Stories followed of thatched cottages and breakfasts of homemade scones and black currant jam, pints in pubs with the locals, and rambles in the countryside.

The next afternoon he appeared with his slides and a second missing button. (Where was Amy? Was she one of the new breed who would throw a man's shirt in his face if he asked her to sew on a button?) The slides were shown in fits and starts, for he used our class time to put them in order. There was an anecdote (Greek: *anekdotos,* unpublished) for each slide. *The Collected Poems* did not come out of the briefcase. In fact, he hadn't even brought his briefcase. While our other classes had become quite interesting, the course I cared the most about appeared to be a failure.

The next afternoon we heard a lecture on Mr. Eliot's life: his work for the bank; his friendship with Mr. Pound; gossip about poor Vivian, his wife; and how Mr. Eliot loved to go dancing. The following day Professor Wally arrived five minutes late but the book was in his hand. My heart bumped against my chest. He smiled at us in a businesslike way and began to read "The Rum Tum Tugger" from Mr. Eliot's *Old Possum's Book of Practical Cats.* He read it with exaggerated expression, grinning at us as he pounded at the rhymes. The class tittered. I had never understood why Mr. Eliot had written such doggerel—if that word can be used for cat poems—even though the poems are clever and would have made him a lot of money if he had lived to see the poems made into a play.

"There now," Professor Wally said. "That wasn't so difficult." He read more cat poems, including "The Ad-dressing of Cats," which led to a long class discussion about a cat's personality versus a dog's. Everyone seemed to have owned one or the other and feelings ran high. Before we left, he announced, "Since tomorrow is our last class, I want each of you to do some homework for me. Make up a cat poem and we'll read the best ones out loud." Everyone groaned, but they were pleased at the prospect of having their poems read in the same classroom in which they had heard Mr. Eliot's. That night I wrote my letter. You can tell how disappointed I was and, I'm afraid, a little snappish.

When we handed our papers in the next afternoon, there were plenty of disclaimers, but secretly everyone was proud of what they had written. Professor Wally went over the poems, chuckling and sending approving glances around the room.. He paused only once—when he got to my letter. After reading it, he looked stricken and unprepared, as though he had been bitten by a snake he had never heard of. He put the letter aside and went back to shuffling through the papers. At last several poems were selected and the authors recited their work aloud to much applause and laughter. Some of the poems were really quite clever, but it was hard for me to join in the fun for I had never been so disappointed in my life. I saw Mr. Eliot with his bowler and black umbrella fading away like that routine Jimmy Durante used to do, stepping back farther and farther into a receding spotlight.

At the end of the hour Professor Wally asked, "Who is Dorothy?" I made myself push up my hand. "Please remain after class," he said.

I nodded, conscience-stricken over what I had said in my letter. Could people be expelled from Senior Learners, their records besmirched? "A troublemaker," mine might read, "incorrigible, antigroup."

He sat silently at his desk until all the others had left. Without his usual grin his round cheeks sagged. When I first saw his beard, it seemed an assertion; now it was more like a disguise. The fringe of hair resting on his shoulders was many different lengths. (Did Amy trim it with her manicuring scissors?) I started to apologize, but he waved away my efforts and, standing up, went to the board and wrote: "A full admission of despair tempered by a massive attempt at order." My heart quickened. It was just what I had felt about Mr. Eliot, but couldn't put into words. Professor Wally turned from the board to the classroom with only me in it and began to lecture. He appeared reluctant at first, almost resentful, as though I were prying a secret out of him.

He started with the early poems, pointing out I don't know how many literary allusions, seven at the beginning of just one poem. Eliot, he explained, liked to stress the continuity of culture by including writers who had come before him. The professor spoke of the subtlety of the rhymes or the unsubtlety and the reason for each. By the time he had finished "The Waste Land" (the footnotes were not as important as I had thought), the shadows in the classroom had shifted from one wall to another. His voice was hoarse. Abruptly he said, "I have to take a leak," and strode out of the room. They were the only words he ever spoke directly to me. I crept down the hall to a water fountain. The clock said he had been lecturing for two hours. I felt as if I were a wicked sorcerer who had cast a spell on the poor man. In all decency, I thought, I should release him. He had given me ten times more than I had hoped for. Yet I couldn't bring myself to leave.

When I returned to the classroom, the blackboard was already half covered with notes on "The Four Quartets." He began talking before I could slip into my seat—a little farther back now—for he was like a fire. It was in the "Quartets," of course, that Mr. Eliot spoke so effectively of the terror of having nothing to think about.

Sometimes Professor Wally paced, sometimes he leaned against the blackboard so that when he turned around to begin writing again, there were smudges of chalk on his back as though someone had marked him out for a special destiny. The sun slipped behind the building opposite ours, darkening the classroom. Once Professor Wally slumped into a chair and silently smoked an entire cigarette, although a sign above him read: "No Smoking." I would have taken that pause as a signal the lecture was over, but he had stopped in the middle of a sentence. When the cigarette was finished, he ground it under his heel, leaving a scar on the worn oak floor, and began again. The scar, I thought with a little thrill, would always be there.

My hand ached from writing and my notes were so cramped they were barely legible, but that didn't matter in the least, because inside my head Professor Wally's words had composed themselves into the shape of Mr. Eliot. I could almost see him, his umbrella out of place in the fair weather, his dark suit too heavy for the warm summer evening, a faint line of perspiration where his bowler rested on his forehead. It was dinnertime when Professor Wally snapped his book shut and escaped out the door, leaving me alone in the classroom.

It is peaceful in the silent room. Shadows overprint the writing on the blackboard so that I can no longer make it out. Over the years thousands of students have occupied this classroom. Now it is my turn. I stay as long as I dare. Finally, the fear of a huffy janitor (Latin: Janus, god of doors) bursting into the room and sweeping me out with an enormous broom forces me from my chair.

The tower clock is chiming seven. I recall Mr. Eliot's line about time and the bell burying the day. I walk through the streets of the university town. Against the rising dusk, the lights go on in the professors' houses and in the dormitories where we students live.

Keeping House with Freud

Carlotta Blohm, a psychoanalyst in her early eighties, knows she and David Bradfort, her patient of thirty years, are a vanishing breed—passé, obsolete, done for. You scarcely need to be told about Carlotta. You can picture it all yourself: the cluttered office with the worn black leather couch; Freud incarnate in a faded, autographed photo; a Feininger etching hastily plucked from the walls of her Viennese home before fleeing to America; a file cabinet covered with dust, for David is now her only patient.

The evening before, the phone had rung, a lively sound in the dead house. "Dr. Blohm? I'm afraid I won't be coming anymore." A voice full of guilt. Harriet, her other patient, was a middle-aged woman with a principled stand against makeup, gray hair in a braid that hung to her waist, ragbag clothes, third-world jewelry, and a long string of husbands and lovers; each one with a cause and each one a loser. Question the man and Harriet defended the cause; question the cause and she defended the man. A no-win proposition, and Harriet always the forgiving victim. Harriet had come to Carlotta three years ago. "I could only be analyzed by a woman," she said, but any suggestion made by Carlotta was hurried to the latest lover, pooh-poohed, boxed, and buried. Under other circumstances, Carlotta would not have been sorry to see Harriet go. No getting away from the fact, though, that Harriet constituted fifty percent of Carlotta's practice. With Harriet gone, David was all that was left. Carlotta comforted herself with the memory of a comment made years ago at a meeting of the Vienna Psychoanalytical

Society by an eager colleague: "One should really have only one patient." The ultimate analytical goal.

Her remaining patient, David Bradfort, inherited his money early on and never worked a day in his life; that is, he never tried a case or sold a house or took over a company. Luckily, he was one of those rare men who have, along with wealth, superb taste. For David, choosing was never a difficulty or a regret. There was scarcely a room in the museum without one of his exquisite gifts: a Sumerian sculpture, an Exikias vase, Munch woodcuts, a Memling, a Cézanne, paintings from the Blue Rider school, two Hoppers.

David was a slight, rather pale man, not a man to spend time out-of-doors, preferring nature *morte*, all imperfections removed. He was shy, but not in the way many people are shy, feeling themselves at the center of things, and therefore, embarrassed to be so much in the spotlight. David was—in all things but his taste in art—diffident, deprecatory, self-conscious, fainthearted, irresolute, and often inarticulate. It was difficult for him to disagree with anyone, and when he did, it was in a manner so civil and vague as not to be noticed. Because of this he had few intimate friendships and had not married.

It was his timidity and apprehension that brought him, thirty years ago, to see Carlotta. He chose Carlotta because she was a European. David, who had spent his youth in prewar Paris, considered Europeans more subtle than Americans, more aware of history. He found he didn't have to begin at the beginning with them, and they were seldom optimistic (a condition he found not only untenable, but tiresome).

There is no reason to believe that just because Carlotta had continued to see David five times a week for thirty years, no goals had been set. Years before, she had promised herself that should David, with his *Befangenheitneurose,* his pathological shyness, finally speak his mind outside of her office, he would no longer be in need of her help. On that day she would begin to terminate his analysis. Perhaps it was something she should have done long ago? When she attended the meetings of the Psychoanalytical Society, where problems with analysands were discussed, she was accused of creating in David a dependency. "Look at your own feelings," they said. "It's a classic case of countertransference. You need him as much as he needs you." Yet Carlotta believed there were people like David who could not bear alone what they found in life. It must be discussed, considered, just as upon seeing extraordinary news on television—a devastating earthquake, the assassination of a president—you ran to the telephone to ask someone, "Are you watching? Did you see it?" That was how it was with David. He came five times a week to ask, "Are you watching? Have you seen it?" And she listened.

Now Carlotta was confronted with the frightening possibility that David might be cured. Carlotta was appalled at the way she was putting it. Surely curing him should be her goal; yet how to face a life without patients? How to give up her search, her last chance to learn the secret which, in spite of her probing, had eluded her and for which she had been looking all of her life? People came to her spilling out banal, ugly, incredible, and even interesting things about themselves, but something was always missing. Left out.

Carlotta could not bear to think of giving David up. Her friends were far away—Graz, San Diego. Her husband, Bernhard, was dead, and even Flegel, the last in what had been a successive series of cats, had been discovered in Carlotta's office, stiff and cold beneath the black leather couch—suffocated, perhaps, by the accumulation of frustrations and dark secrets that had spilled over and now lurked there like a black tide.

That morning, just before David had settled himself on the couch, she had seen how he noted the position of the box of Kleenex and the white linen towel on which his head rested. A meticulous observer of details, he must have noticed they were exactly as he had left them the day before. Carlotta admonished herself for not straightening things up. He would guess he was her only patient. Rats deserting a sinking ship? Would he panic and run for shore himself? No. He lay down, straightened his coat, took one of the *Makronen* she had made for him, and said, "I'm afraid I've been thinking of Paris."

Carlotta understood The Presence had returned. When David was upset, he imagined (she was sure it was his imagination, for she was not a disciple of Jung) a kind of presence at his bedside which he described variously as a crouching animal, a person without a face, or sometimes a vacant spot where there was absolutely nothing at all. David escaped from this apparition by dwelling on a place where he had been happy; often it was the Paris of the early thirties, where, after

Harvard, he had lived for several years. On this day he had recalled his
first apartment in the faubourg of Saint-Germain-des-Près on the rue de
Grenelle. He spoke wistfully of strolls through the Parc Monceau, the
plane trees in leaf along the quays, the oaks and chestnuts in the Bois.

"Very bucolic," Carlotta had said, cutting him off, knowing the dangers of allowing a patient to escape to something pleasant.

"I didn't mean to make it sound merely pastoral," he apologized. "It
was very civilized. I might spend an afternoon with Étienne Lévy in his
shop. The Louis XVI secrétaire at the museum came from him and two
or three pieces I have at home. I remember the excitement of carrying
my first Picasso to Monsieur Bac's on the rue Bonaparte to choose
exactly the right frame."

She saw he was surreptitiously trying to remove from his bridgework
a bit of coconut. To give him time, she asked, "When you think of
Paris, there is usually a reason?" The least suggestion of anger created
in David guilt, which turned into The Presence by his bedside. It was
an old problem. How often she had told him, "Anger can be healthy.
The God of both your religion and mine has lost his temper. Surely you
don't put yourself above him."

Finally, in a barely audible voice David said, "They want to sell my
Cézanne. Well, of course, I must admit it's no longer mine. I gave it to
the museum years ago."

She knew at once which painting David meant. She knew the history
of all his gifts to the museum: the galleries at which they had been
discovered, their provenance, the excitement of carrying them off.
They were the only love affairs he had to bring to the analysis. The
Cézanne was a still life with two lemons and an orange. She thought
from its colors and shapes, its harmony and balance, someone could
create a perfect world. It was the strength of her own indignation that
suggested to Carlotta that David's anger might effect a cure. "How
could that be?" was all she permitted herself.

"They want to buy a Dwork. Ours is the only major museum in the
country without one. The Kurtain Gallery has sent one on approval.
Hunter refers to it as both 'seminal' and 'major,' his ultimate accolades.
I believe it all started when *Art News* warned Dwork prices were going
through the ceiling. Hunter knows the acquisitions fund doesn't have
that kind of money." Hunter was the director of the museum, one of

those sorry men who hunger for recognition and immortality while recognizing their own mediocrity. "If you don't know your limitations, you can still hope," David had once said, "but Hunter hopes while knowing it's impossible. You have to feel sorry for the man."

"Who is this Dwork?" Carlotta asked. "And what is his work like?"

"Dwork paints with spray cans, mops, pushbrooms, shovels. He doesn't know what painting is. As for the Cézanne, they think it won't matter if they lose it. They count on getting the three Cézannes from my collection when I'm dead."

The thought that David had come at last to the provocation that would cause him to assert himself both cheered and saddened her. If he were cured, what would she do with her mornings?—could she even bring herself to get out of bed? In Vienna she had a great aunt, who at age seventy-five, announced there was nothing in the world any longer worth getting up for—a Proust who did not write. As long as David appeared each day, Carlotta was an analyst. She could read her journals, prepare her notes, occupy her office; could refer, with only a slight exaggeration, to her "patients"; could think about someone besides herself, the dreariest topic she knew; and so she hedged a little. "Have you seen the painting?"

"I can't bring myself to look at it. Of course, I've seen illustrations of his work. But the selling of the Cézanne is not the only problem. If they get rid of that painting, what might they do with all the other things I've given? I can see my gifts flying, one by one, out of the windows of the museum, sucked away by the vacuum in Hunter's head. Even worse, all the works of art I've chosen so carefully to go to the museum when I die might be replaced over the years by the ugly accidents of media stars. The trustees' meeting is tonight and I've a good notion to tell them exactly what I think. And yet . . ."

"And yet?" In spite of herself these last words cheered her.

"Once I was thought avant-garde myself. When I bought my Munchs, they were considered grotesque, as decadent as Dwork."

She wrestled her personal feelings, like a tiger, to the floor. "Under the circumstances," she said, "many people would be angry." Before she could correct her high-minded gesture, the hour was over, and she saw with dismay how her suggestion would accompany David to the trustees' meeting.

Before leaving the office, David paused and, taking a small package from his pocket, said in his mannered way, "I read in the paper that you will be honored with a *Festschrift* this evening by the Psychoanalytical Society. I hope you will allow me to give you this." He thrust the package at her, blushed, and hurried out before she could challenge him.

Here was something to cling to: David's behavior was unprofessional. The gift would have to be returned and his gesture worked through. Whatever he did at the trustees' meeting tonight, the examination of his motives in giving her a present would take time. Still, it had been a long while since she had received a gift and she could not stop herself from opening it. A small porcelain box—Meissen, probably eighteenth century—with gold mounts. On the cover and sides of the box were exquisitely painted Japanese children at play. There were birds, a swing, a dog romping through flowers. All the children were smiling.

From the moment she saw the box she knew she would never surrender it. It was the kind of possession that immediately becomes a talisman, gathering around itself indisputable power. If she were to keep the gift, she could hardly ask David to consider his motives in giving it. So that excuse was gone. But the gift itself, its choice: a box, children, games. There was a wealth of material there—weeks, perhaps months.

The psychoanalysts invited to the *Festschrift* banquet celebrating Carlotta's fifty years in the practice of analysis were surprised, even a little irritated, to find her alive and still seeing patients.

They remembered her from the days when Freud was in his ascendancy. Carlotta would stride into the meeting of the Psychoanalytical Society, the only woman and the only lay analyst among men and doctors, carrying her briefcase, in the days before women carried briefcases, as though it were a heavy suitcase. After firm handshakes all around, Carlotta settled onto the least comfortable chair, both feet placed firmly on the ground, not crossed or close together in the feminine guarding position, but apart. No one would want to? No one would dare? Yet she was a woman, no one more so. She opened the briefcase and, nestled among the copious notes that explained one life after another, lay an enormous *Apfel Strudel*. Talk of neurosis, narcissism, hysteria, and premature ejaculation was accompanied by mur-

murs of delight from doctors, whose fingers were sticky with apple juice and whose mustaches and beards trembled with tender flakes of the best homemade strudel this side of the Atlantic.

Carlotta had fled Austria in the thirties, bringing Freud's gospel to the Midwest. So orthodox had she been in the treatment of her patients, some swore you could smell Freud's cigar smoke in her office. The analysts at the banquet who had trained under her recalled her vehement outcries against anything that deviated from the master's teaching: transactional analysis, biofeedback, gestalt therapy, behavior modification. She considered it all nonsense, reserving her greatest indignation for Jung, whom she called "that overwrought man with the mandalas."

Carlotta, feeling ancient and over with, nevertheless greeted the guests with a smile that tried to suggest survival was everything. She was wearing a silk dress purchased especially for the occasion. Arranged over her substantial frame it had, like all her dresses with their shapeless tops and awkward length, the look of a thirties housedress. Her red hair was a rusty gray now, but still braided in old-fashioned whorls like wispy earmuffs. Behind her gold wire glasses darted quick glances, taken from the side of the head like a bird—a result of years of wary, evaluating, oblique looks at the supine patient. Lies? Cover-up? Repressed material? Or at least—it hadn't happened in fifty years—the truth.

Carlotta was embarrassed at the number of names she couldn't recall. Had they sent tickets helter-skelter to pad the attendance? It was a relief to see the period of bizarre clothes was over—Nehru jackets, Navaho headbands, South American ponchos, and ubiquitous jeans. She must have been thinking aloud because Mark Penfold said, "Don't count your blessings too soon. These three-piece-suit types with the rep ties and alligator loafers are strictly dressing for success. Two hundred dollars an hour to see a patient, and when they luck into the legal system, five hundred for a one-hour deposition; if it goes to trial, several thousand, and another wife-beater or murderer is out on the streets. At least the hippie shrinks were embarrassed by money."

"But by nothing else." Too late she recalled some rumor about Penfold diddling a young girl he was treating.

"You wouldn't have us be judgmental?"

"We accept while we await developments. We start where they are; we don't end there. We are their guides, not their playfellows." If the shoe fit.

"Ah, well," Penfold said, "when it comes down to it, what do we do but move the furniture around a little."

Carlotta was shocked.

Norman Diamond, in a Pierre Cardin suit and Roman emperor hairstyle, came to guide Carlotta to the speakers' table where a fruit cup was waiting—turgid pears and slippery peaches. They weren't going first class: she was too old and powerless; her letters of recommendation would get them nothing; the people she could influence were dead. Still, it was nice of them to come here, and she beamed a smile in the general direction of the guests who had reluctantly left the bar and were now showing a general air of dissatisfaction with their tablemates: they shared the same professional building and had coffee together five days a week, so nothing new could be expected there, unless someone were to recount the latest divorce settlement horror story, and who needed that?

Dessert, a pale, weeping sherbet, was over and Diamond was on his feet, his high-pitched electronic voice zinging over the clatter of dishes, as waitresses snatched coffee cups from guests trying to hang on to them, like sleepy children struggling to take a toy to bed. "Dr. Blohm, colleagues, we are here today—*tonight,* I should say . . ."—a little pause while Diamond, ever-conscientious, tried to figure out the meaning behind his slip of the tongue. Not too serious, evidently, because with a little complicit smile at Carlotta—even *we* have these lapses—he continued, "to honor one of our own.

"Who among us can say he or she has not been influenced by Dr. Blohm in the course of his or her (Carlotta shuddered at the glut of pronouns) profession? We have read her scholarly articles in our journals, attended her lectures, heard her astute, perceptive comments at the meetings of the Psychoanalytical Society, and some of us have been fortunate enough to have been under . . . (another thoughtful pause) *with* Dr. Blohm as an analysand." An arch smile arrowed toward her.

It had been thirty years since Norman Diamond had lain on her couch. In those days she had had more requests from prospective analysands than she could accommodate. It was to be a dynasty: Freud had

laid hands on her and she would anoint others. A royal line. Diamond
had pleaded to be analyzed by her; she was the only one for whom he
held any respect. She gave him eight o'clock in the morning. Gratefully
he agreed, but he was not an early riser and often came to her home,
where her office was located, in pajamas: paisley silk or, more likely,
rayon. In any case, unwashable. She was appalled at the extravagance
and the unhygienic aspect of his sleepware. Perhaps because of the
pajamas, he brought with him numerous dreams, still warm from the
bed. Diamond had not trusted her with the dreams but sifted them first
through his own repressed and unimaginative mind, finally handing
them over, like a cat laying a dead bird on the doorstoop—the lively
struggle over, nothing left to examine but a few broken bones and a bit
of blood.

He had been in love with Carlotta, a woman of fifty, while he was in
his thirties. Transference, of course, and they eventually worked it
through. Did he recall how, when he heard her husband, Bernhard,
moving overhead in his preparations to leave for the university, Diamond would writhe with jealousy, blurting out, uncensored at last,
dreams in which a thinly disguised Bernhard suffered hideous
accidents—was run over, beheaded, burned to a cinder? When this was
uncovered, Diamond was dismayed at his suppressed rage, pounding
his head, rolling his eyes, trying to laugh it off. Ten years ago, when
Bernhard had died and Norman Diamond was fifteen years out of his
analysis, he had sent at least fifty dollars worth of flowers to the funeral
home. At that price the florist had thrown in a little of everything: Fiji
mums, bird of paradise, red and yellow gladiolas. What was meant to
express sympathy took on the look of celebration.

Diamond was introducing Gerald Green, who was to make the jokes.
Carlotta knew the term "roast" and waited for the knife. Dinners hon-
oring people were now like those racks of "contemporary" birthday
cards people sent, choosing, perhaps wisely, insults over sentimentality. Bernhard, dead and defenseless, was the first target. "We all remember Carlotta's (no more Dr. Blohm—the gloves were off) charming
(how Bernhard would have hated the word) husband. Someone at the
university once asked him what his wife did and he said, 'She listens
all day to dirty stories.' "

The anecdote was apocryphal, but close to the bone. Bernhard had never approved of her work. "All that talk, that *Geschwätzigkeit,* is embarrassing. Have those people no pride, pouring out their private thoughts to a stranger? How can you listen to such things day after day?" Once, coming home late together from some university function, they had driven by a cemetery. Moving around the tombstones were dark shapes carrying flashlights. Alarmed by the eerie sight, she had turned to Bernhard: "What is it?"

"They're pulling worms out of the ground to sell to fishermen. They collect thousands in an evening. I understand it's very profitable. Your kinsmen, *nicht?*"

Yet Bernhard had been a compassionate man. Probably he could not bear to think of people in misery, people filling his home with tales of unloving mothers, lustful fathers, husbands and wives betrayed. He had avoided the study where she saw her patients: it might have been some chamber of horrors, where blood and bits of corpses lay strewn about.

Green was reaching for laughs. "There is no truth to that rumor that Carlotta is still seeing the patients she started out with fifty years ago." He was talking about David Bradfort. Knowing David might soon leave her, Carlotta appreciated the irony. Let Green have his little joke. He understood as well as she did that years of neurosis could not be undone in an hour. You had to unravel the string, get at the knots. Everyone knew Green himself was a holdout, practically a permanent fixture on Irving Schwartz's couch, because Green would not face up to the phobia which caused him to climb ten flights of stairs to his office every day rather than take an elevator.

As Carlotta knew he would, Green was dredging up her habit of giving refreshments to her patients. Had her Viennese credentials been a little less impressive, say only a few weeks with Freud rather than nearly two years, she would have been thrown out of the analytical society for this eccentricity long ago. A hundred times they had asked her how she could maintain impersonal relationships with her patients when she fed them coffeecake and cookies. Impossible, they said, insisting she work it through. She explained that the patients came to her home and were, therefore, not only her patients but her guests. And so, over the years there beside her couch the patient found *Strudel, Stollen, Kugelhupfe,* and *Plünderflechten*—all homemade. "In no time," Green was saying, "her patients would begin to dream of being locked in a pastry shop with the baker."

At last she was on her feet, about to sum up fifty years of psychoanalytical practice. As she looked out at her colleagues and thought of how many of their secrets she had listened to over the years, she had a momentary vision of visitation of small, obscene birds hovering just over their heads. She thought, so this is what God must bear. Hurriedly she launched into her speech, giving them what they expected—some adulatory references to Freud, a few sycophantic words for those who had arranged the *Festschrift* affair, and a sentimental mention of the old days, when their profession (craft? obsession?) was at its peak.

Carlotta saw they were not listening—thinking, perhaps, of their investment portfolios or a seminar she had heard them discussing on the psychoanalytical aspects of terrorism; the seminar was to take place on a cruise down the Nile. It was global problems that engaged them now: man himself was only mildly interesting. His aberrations were not only acceptable, they were the most interesting thing about him—hardly something to be investigated and eradicated. She hurried through her concluding remarks and graciously accepted the collection of papers written by her colleagues to honor her. There was time for only a cursory flipping of pages of the somewhat slim volume. A title caught her eye: "The Implications of Rodent Pets During the Latent Years." She was in no hurry to read the papers. Carlotta thought of David's exquisite gift, and what he might have said to the trustees while she had been sitting through Green's jokes.

Driving home through the dark streets, she carried her gloomy thoughts with her. They had all but buried her at the *Festschrift* banquet. She hurried to her front door where a bright light burned. The house was in a small island of five or six streets of large old homes adrift in a decaying section of the city. For Sale signs proliferated. Lawns went untrimmed, and a few houses were actually abandoned. Someone her age did not dare walk about, even in the daytime. A year ago her home had been burglarized. They had taken the television (it had been gone two months before Carlotta had noticed) and some silver (presents from her and Bernhard's twenty-fifth anniversary). She was glad to be rid of the polishing chore. Her first editions of Freud were untouched, but unaccountably stolen—and badly missed—were her 78 r.p.m. records: Schweitzer's Bach preludes and Casel's Bach suites with the dust of real gold on the labels, a testimony to their prewar quality. She had still played them on her old Magnavox, a wedding gift from Bernhard. She liked to believe that somewhere her records were changing the lives of those who had stolen them, but she knew better. It would be the fate of the records to be forever traded or sold, and no one would ever listen to them again.

In the middle of the night she awoke, turned on the bedside lamp, and—according to the instructions given to her personally by Professor Freud over fifty years before—wrote down her dream. Her self-analysis never ended, and often it made her miserable. In the course of a day she would do things which appeared suitable, even nice; then she would examine her deeds, only to find her motives selfish, occasionally mischievous. She avoided the word "evil," for it suggested the corollary, "good". "Good" was simplistic. Yet she had witnessed evil. Like David, she tried to get rid of her night thoughts by recalling pleasanter times. She retraced her early morning walk through the Vienna streets to Berggasse 9, Professor Freud's apartment over the butcher shop. She climbed the stairway; saw Freud's housekeeper, Paula Fichtl, discreet but welcoming, answer the door; heard Freud's chows barking in the distance; saw once again the Professor's study, with its couch covered by a Turkish rug, velvet cushions, and a blanket. She felt the dry firmness of the Professor's handshake that began each *Stunde*. She basked again in the undivided attention of the Professor—the encouragement, the support, the insight. It was like being under God's gaze, as though for the moment you were the only person on earth. When you left, you carried that singularity with you and were amazed that others did not find you as fascinating as the Professor had.

Only a few blocks from the Professor, at Berggasse 19, were the quarters of the Vienna Psychoanalytical Society. The members met in newly decorated rooms with handsome red drapes and wall coverings and comfortable chairs, the height of bourgeois fashion, while they were all confuting the bourgeoisie. There were intense arguments, with the *Gemütlichkeit* of coffee and cakes afterward. Or they would all go to the Reiss-Bar off the Kärntnerstrasse, and there, seated around ornate tables of gilt wood and marble, they would prolong their discussions, accusing the old enemies—Adler, Stekel, Jung, Bleuler, and Reich—men who had dared challenge the master.

Little was said about what was going on in Germany. There was only incredulity when they heard that the Archduke Otto von Hapsburg had offered to take over the chancellorship from the vacillating Schuschnigg. After all, Bruno Walter, a Jew, had had his conductor's contract with the Vienna Opera renewed. But in no time Schuschnigg himself was on the radio, telling them either Hitler would choose their chancellor, or the German army would march into Austria.

At the last meeting of the Psychoanalytical Society—held on that cold Sunday afternoon in March, the day after Hitler had come to Vienna—Anna Freud had chaired the meeting and asked them, one by one, what they planned to do, and one by one they spoke the name of the country to which they would go. Their god had left, too, making his way to England. Carlotta wondered, rather frivolously, if Freud had taken his beloved chows with him, but there was no one now to ask.

She saw where her thoughts of Vienna had taken her and gave up on sleeping to wander through the darkened house to the kitchen, where she made up a batch of *Wienerbrot* for David. The dough was soft and malleable, with just enough resistance to make her feel she was not doing all the work herself.

The next morning Carlotta read the headline on the front page of the newspaper: "Museum Benefactor Threatens Withdrawal of Bequest." Hunter had, as predicted, spoken of Dwork's "seminal and major" work. He regretted the loss of the Cézanne, but "the opportunity could not be passed up. And there would be (here he probably cast a coy look at David) more and better (could he have said that? Yes) Cézannes to come."

And David's response. She knew what he would be experiencing— the palpitations, the rapid breathing, the tremors. "If you sell the Cézanne, I will go immediately to my lawyer and change my bequest to the museum. My entire collection will be left elsewhere." "Elsewhere"—Carlotta thought that was a nice touch. The faintest echo of the British aristocrat.

Hunter in abashed retreat. "Misunderstanding . . . I had no idea . . . no need to carry this further . . . it goes without saying the Dwork will be returned." A rout. Carlotta congratulated herself. It had taken thirty years, but David had spoken out. Firmly. And on a crucial issue. Or was it Hunter who had effected the cure? Perhaps all David had needed was sufficient provocation? Perhaps, Carlotta thought, she had been merely shielding him all these years from what was needed?

In any event, David's analysis was over. She would allow a few weeks for an orderly rounding off—there was still his gift to work through—and then terminate. What a word. And their relationship of thirty years? How to terminate that? Could not two people who knew one another so well—better than most married couples (for she was not fool enough to believe so perceptive and sensitive a man as David had not known what was going on in her mind, as well as she knew what was going on in his)—couldn't two such people simply become friends, and the devil with professional ethics? But the Elohistic picture of Freud looked down upon her, and she knew she could never let herself do anything so unprofessional.

By the time David arrived for his appointment and was munching appreciatively on the *Wienerbrot,* Carlotta was able to appear almost enthusiastic. "I saw it in the paper. You were very firm with them."

"At least I tried to be."

"You must give yourself credit. You won your point. You stood up to them."

"All thanks to you," David said graciously.

"And now we must think about making an ending of the analysis." It sounded like a kind of slaughter. "You have accomplished the goal we set many years ago."

"I'm afraid there has been a small setback," David murmured.

Carlotta leaned forward. Over the years she had discovered his quietness was in direct proportion to the importance of his material.

"I stopped to look at the Dwork as I left the meeting, just to be sure I hadn't been unjust."

"And?"

"It was even more crude, more vulgar and hideous, than I imagined. The painting was huge—at least fourteen or fifteen feet long. Obviously Dwork felt his work was strong enough to be extended, magnified. Or perhaps he believed if he made the painting enormous, people would have to think it important, like those pictures of a microscopic drop of water, in which innocuous creatures, now enlarged, take on an impressive but spurious importance. The painting was haphazard, slap-dash, a pastiche of accidental effects and incompatible colors. It had no plan, no subtlety, no guiding intelligence; the artist was nowhere in the painting."

"So you felt quite justified in your position."

"I did, but unfortunately there was a regression." David rose slightly from the couch, took a bite of the bread and a sip of coffee. He lowered himself back onto the familiar and receptive indentations of the couch. "This morning I called the Kurtain gallery in New York and bought the Dwork for the museum. I will have to sell two or three things to get the money, but there will be no serious gaps, no major losses from my collection."

"You gave it to them?" For once Carlotta could not keep incredulity from her voice.

"I'm afraid it would seem so. I suppose I did gain my point about the Cézanne, and I've had my lawyers word my bequest so that nothing can be disposed of in the future. But, unhappily, the Dwork is on the way." David rolled his eyes back to get a glimpse of Carlotta. She was gazing fondly down at him, the mother whose child has an adorable weakness.

ILLINOIS SHORT FICTION

Crossings by Stephen Minot
A Season for Unnatural Causes by Philip F. O'Connor
Curving Road by John Stewart
Such Waltzing Was Not Easy by Gordon Weaver

Rolling All the Time by James Ballard
Love in the Winter by Daniel Curley
To Byzantium by Andrew Fetler
Small Moments by Nancy Huddleston Packer

One More River by Lester Goldberg
The Tennis Player by Kent Nelson
A Horse of Another Color by Carolyn Osborn
The Pleasures of Manhood by Robley Wilson, Jr.

The New World by Russell Banks
The Actes and Monuments by John William Corrington
Virginia Reels by William Hoffman
Up Where I Used to Live by Max Schott

The Return of Service by Jonathan Baumbach
On the Edge of the Desert by Gladys Swan
Surviving Adverse Seasons by Barry Targan
The Gasoline Wars by Jean Thompson

Desirable Aliens by John Bovey
Naming Things by H. E. Francis
Transports and Disgraces by Robert Henson
The Calling by Mary Gray Hughes

Into the Wind by Robert Henderson
Breaking and Entering by Peter Makuck
The Four Corners of the House by Abraham Rothberg
Ladies Who Knit for a Living by Anthony E. Stockanes

Pastorale by Susan Engberg
Home Fires by David Long
The Canyons of Grace by Levi Peterson
Babaru by B. Wongar

Bodies of the Rich by John J. Clayton
Music Lesson by Martha Lacy Hall
Fetching the Dead by Scott R. Sanders
Some of the Things I Did Not Do by Janet Beeler Shaw

Honeymoon by Merrill Joan Gerber
Tentacles of Unreason by Joan Givner
The Christmas Wife by Helen Norris
Getting to Know the Weather by Pamela Painter

Birds Landing by Ernest Finney
Serious Trouble by Paul Friedman
Tigers in the Wood by Rebecca Kavaler
The Greek Generals Talk by Phillip Parotti

Singing on the Titanic by Perry Glasser
Legacies by Nancy Potter
Beyond This Bitter Air by Sarah Rossiter
Scenes from the Homefront by Sara Vogan

Tumbling by Kermit Moyer
Water into Wine by Helen Norris
The Trojan Generals Talk by Phillip Parotti
Playing with Shadows by Gloria Whelan